THE
ARRANGEMENT

M. RAVENEL

The Arrangement
(The Plainclothes Tootsie Mysteries – book 1)

Printed in the United States of America

ISBN: 978-1-7364913-0-0 (Ebook)
ISBN: 978-0-9837719-9-9 (Paperback)

10 9 8 7 6 5 4 3 2 1

THE
ARRANGEMENT

CHAPTER 1

Bronx, New York, 1975

I peered through the slats of the blinds covering the glass on my office door and watched the dark, brooding man in the hallway. Sporting a neatly trimmed horseshoe mustache and wearing a burgundy polyester leisure suit, the man appeared to be in his late twenties. He stood every bit of six-foot-three under the fluorescent lights, which hummed and flickered, casting a hazy glow over the glistening beads of sweat on his brow. The man scrutinized me with an unsteady gaze. He shifted his thin frame from one foot to the other, repeatedly clasping and unclasping his perfectly manicured hands. His fidgeting reminded me of a paranoid junkie on the run from the law or a frazzled tourist who'd just encountered one of New York City's infamous giant rodents.

Once I'd watched him squirm long enough, I said, "Yes?"

"Ah, hello, Miss. I'm looking for Detective Carter," he replied in a low, muffled voice.

I discreetly slid one of the dead bolt latches aside. "What business do you have with Detective Carter?"

The man blinked. "I, uh… want to hire him. This *is* his office, right?" His gaze lowered to the inscription on the door. "T. Carter, Private Detective?"

I slid aside another latch. "It is."

"You his secretary or something?"

I snorted. The good-looking fool had jokes. Not like I could blame him for the mistake. New York City had become a cesspool of crime and punishment with no end in sight. And it was certainly no place for a proper lady to be getting her hands all dirty doing gritty, unsavory detective work.

I unhooked a chain latch, the third and final lock, and opened the door. The man's thick eyebrows rose slightly.

"Detective Carter does not have a secretary, but she's willing to listen to your case." I stepped aside and gestured him in.

His mouth opened slowly then closed.

"Look, either come in or beat it. I'm closing this door in three seconds. This building's had three attempted robberies this week already."

After another round of hesitation, he clenched his jaw then finally entered.

"Have a seat." I shut the door and swiveled its window blinds closed.

The man remained where he stood. His head moved from left to right as he scanned my two-room office, which was dimly lit by the green banker's lamp sitting on my paper-strewn wooden desk. A few filing cabinets lined the walls beside the desk, and a wooden bookshelf was tucked into one corner. The double-hung window behind the desk overlooked Leland Avenue from the fourth floor's fire escape. For a moment, the man's attention settled on the view of the city's nighttime lights.

The building, which had been used for residential housing back in the '20s and '30s, had since been converted into offices for small businesses. I was one of the lucky few to be on good, friendly terms with Sam Contreras, the landlord, who essentially allowed me to live where I worked. It was the best of both worlds, especially when there was no way I was able to afford rent for both an apartment and office space. Not only was I a good tenant, but Sam was less stressed having a former cop around. For added pressure, he used my residence as an excuse for not hiring a doorman for the building. That would-be money knocked twenty-five dollars off my rent for every time I thwarted a robbery in the building. So far, at the rate things were going, I was on my way to earning a free month. But despite the money and how good it felt to stop criminals in their tracks, I was only one person. I wished Sam would stop being such a cheapskate.

I plopped down in my creaky desk chair and leaned back. "If you're done casing the joint, how about we talk a little business?"

"Ah…" He rubbed the back of his head, his face full of confusion.

I glanced at the clock above the front door. *7:40. Sweet Saint Mary,* this was going to be a long night. "Yeah, that's right. I've got the wrong equipment in my pants. But them's the breaks. So if I ain't what you're looking for, then you can just step on out that door."

He perked up at that. "Whoa. Hey, now, I'm cool with—"

"It's written all over your face."

He cleared his throat. "I apologize."

"Right. So now that we got that out of the way, how about you tell me who you are and why you're here." I gestured to the empty chair in front of my desk. It was one of those hard wooden school chairs that made a person's rear feel like a numb flapjack after only five minutes of sitting. I'd picked up the chair at a secondhand shop for a buck. It kept prospective clients from getting too long-winded.

He looked at the chair a moment, like there might be a bear trap in the seat. Then he edged closer and rested his hands on the back of it, drumming those nervous fingers on the wood, but he still didn't sit.

Geez Louise. This guy was jumpier than a liar on a witness stand. That meant he probably had an interesting case. The jumpy ones usually did. In my eight years of solving cases, I'd developed a soft spot for the nervous Nellies.

"My name is Gregory Miles. My wife, Luanda"—the finger-drumming ramped up to machine-gun speed—"has gone missing…"

I opened my desk drawer and pulled a pocket-sized notepad out from under one of my stashed Dick Tracy comic books. I plucked a freshly sharpened pencil from the coffee can sitting on my desk and jotted some notes. "Have you gone to the police?"

"Actually, yeah. The chief at the Fifty-Fourth Precinct told me to come to you."

I raised my eyebrows. "He did, did he?"

"Yeah. And…" He fished through the breast pocket of his blazer and pulled out a Tootsie Roll Midgee. "He told me to give you this. Said you would know what it meant."

I cracked a smile, taking the small piece of candy. It was swell of Chief Lewis to always look out for me like that. I'd known Rob since I was a kid, when he'd just started out on the force as a beat cop. These days, with the police being in high demand because of all the crime and protests, there were few resources available for small-time cases like Mr. Miles's.

I put the piece of candy with the others that filled a medium-sized glass jar on my desk. Call it a strange infatuation, or perhaps childhood nostalgia, but Tootsie Rolls were my sweet addiction. I was like a chain-smoker that went through five packs a day. Indulging in a Tootsie Roll or two was the perfect way to brighten up a stressful day, and, boy, did this job come with plenty of them.

"Yes, I know exactly what it means, and you came to the right place." I lightly tapped the tip of my pencil against the notepad. "Now, back to your missing wife."

"Yes." His face went pale again, and he white-knuckled the back of the chair. "Luanda is such a wonderful woman. She's tall and beautiful, and she would give a movie star like Pam Grier a run for her money."

"Pretty bold statement, Mr. Miles," I said flatly.

He shrugged. "I may be a little biased."

"When was the last time you saw your wife?"

"Two days ago. Monday morning, around four, before I went to work. I'm a mail sorter at the post office. Luanda works three days a week part-time at Marlene's Diner over on Webster Avenue. If she works the first shift, I usually see her when I come home in the afternoon. If it's the second shift, I'll see her when she gets home around ten o'clock that night. It's our usual weekly routine."

"You two sound like the typical happily married couple," I said. *Maybe a little* too *happy.*

"We sure are. Our five-year wedding anniversary is coming up in two weeks. We're going to take a cruise to Bermuda."

"Bermuda, eh? Fancy."

He snorted. "Yeah, and expensive. But only the best for my Luanda."

"So what changed in your usual weekly routine?" I steered the conversation back on track.

"Well…" He moistened his lips. "Luanda is a doll, putting in extra hours at work so she could help pitch in with the trip's expenses. I kept telling her she didn't have to do that, but she insisted. So I let her do her thing. As a result, she'd often come home late from her second shift, many times well after midnight. Some nights, I was asleep by the time she returned, so I never got a chance to see her."

"Did she ever call and let you know she was going to be home late?" I asked.

"Sometimes she did. But there were times when the diner got slammed, and she was so busy that she forgot to call."

"Fair enough. Go on."

"Monday, when I came home, she wasn't there. Her purse was gone, too, so I figured she went into work early. I called the diner, but no one there had seen her all day. Later that night, I went down to the diner in person but saw no sign of her. I stayed up later than I should, waiting for her at home, but she never came back. Tuesday, I asked around at the diner again, but no one had still seen her. I called around town to places she might've gone, but no dice. I gave her one more sleepless night to come back, and when she didn't, I went straight to the police. And here I am."

"Yeah. Here you are." My pencil moved steadily as I took careful notes. "Why didn't you call the police sooner?"

He shrugged. "I don't know. I thought maybe she worked herself so much she might've been too tired to come home, so she stayed over with one of her girlfriends instead."

"She would've called you if that were the case, right?"

"Yeah, I suppose. Depending on how late she would've gotten in from work."

I lifted an eyebrow. "You don't sound very sure of yourself."

His face hardened. "Hey, I love her with all my heart. I trust her and give her all the freedom she wants. I'm not some jealous husband who goes checking on his wife every five minutes, if that's what you're thinking."

"All right, all right, I dig it. I just need to cover all possibilities." I flipped to a new page of my notebook. "Were there any signs of a break-in? Anything missing or out of place?"

"None. The only thing missing was her purse."

"You *sure* she doesn't have any other men in her life?" I asked, thinking about the unfathomable number of infidelity cases I'd dealt with in the past.

His eyes widened. "Hell no! I spoil her like a queen. I do everything I can to be a perfect husband to her. She's got no reason to go looking elsewhere."

I stopped scribbling and looked up from the pad, remembering some of my earlier cases. Spoiling a highly attractive woman was usually a recipe for disaster. "You mentioned she had girlfriends."

"Yeah, some women friends from the diner."

"And none of them had seen her?"

He shook his head and sighed.

I tapped the eraser end of my pencil against my lips as I scanned my notes. "And she's never been gone this long before?"

"Yeah. Crazy, ain't it? I just don't get it. I'm worried as hell about her. She means everything to me."

"I'm sure she does, Mr. Miles," I said in a calm, cool tone. "Hypothetically speaking, she could very well have been kidnapped, especially if she allegedly rivals Pam Grier in the looks department." I raised my eyebrows at him dubiously.

His eyes grew wider than saucers. "No!"

"Relax. I was being facetious. I'll take the case. My rate is a hundred seventy-five dollars a day, plus expenses."

Slowly, he pulled his hands back from the chair. Stepping closer to the desk, he fished out two one-hundred-dollar bills from his brown leather wallet. He plunked the money on the desk and slid it toward me. "Can you start tonight?"

I eyed the crisp bills, which still carried a whiff of their newly minted smell. "Totally."

"I just want her back safe and sound. If you find out *anything*, please let me know." He spat out his telephone number.

I jotted it down on my pad, but I had no intentions of contacting him unless absolutely necessary. Otherwise, it would wait until this case was closed. The last thing I needed was to give a client a false sense of hope. "I'll take care of it. In the meantime, you go home and try to relax."

He looked at me with eyes full of hesitation. His Adam's apple bobbed.

"Something else you need to tell me, Mr. Miles?"

"Are you... Are you sure you can do this?"

I raised my eyebrows. "You're wondering if I'm qualified?"

"Ah, well—"

"Save your breath." I gestured to the framed law enforcement and professional investigator certificates hanging prominently by the front door, alongside my business licenses.

His brow furrowed as he scrutinized them one by one. "Rita Carter?"

I grunted. "Call me Tootsie."

"Right on. Those are some impressive achievements. I ain't gonna argue with you—that's for sure. I like your no-nonsense attitude. Just be careful out there, will you? These streets are crazy."

"Your concern is flattering but unnecessary. I wouldn't have been working this gig for the past eight years if I didn't know the rules of the streets. If I were you, I'd worry less about me and more about getting *yourself* safely home, you dig?" I rose from my desk, pressing my palms flat on the top.

He opened his mouth to reply, closed it, then gave me an absent nod. "Yeah... I'll leave you to it, then. Goodnight, Ms. Carter—or should I say, Detective."

"Whatever floats your boat." I opened the door and let him out. He stepped into the hallway, timidly rubbing his hands together again and looking over his shoulder at me with trepidation. I closed the door and reset the locks. If he knew what was good for him, he would jet out of there faster than a rocket-powered Mustang. Night was coming, and that was when the crazies would come out and play. A clean-cut, well-dressed cat like him would be easy pickings for a gang of lowlife suckers.

In any event, it was time to get started on his case. I left my office and went through a door that led to the tenement's one and only bedroom. Its minuscule size made a dollhouse feel like a mansion. But I'd somehow managed to make it work out with having a place to sleep and a place for my clothes, and I'd even fit in a makeshift kitchenette, complete with a mini fridge and hotplate for cooking.

I squeezed past my daybed and opened the armoire. I retrieved my favorite pair of tiny gold hoop earrings from the jewelry box, and then switched out my casual shoes for my black steel-toe boots. Not only were these babies good for walking, they were also great for dealing with fools who tried to get fresh.

After a quick check in the hanging wall mirror, I returned to my office and gathered my essentials: my wallet, my snub-nosed Colt .38, my pocket-sized notebook, a couple of Tootsie Rolls, a set of handcuffs, a pair of black leather gloves, and lastly, my old police badge. I'd only been on the force for three years, straight out of high school, before resigning. I'd found out the hard way that the cop life was a far cry from what my childhood hero Dick Tracy did. Instead of cool car chases, shootouts, and drug busts, I was stuck behind a switchboard, typewriter, or coffee maker all day. Promotion wasn't even an option for me, I had later learned. Added to that was the fact that female officers were treated poorly by their male peers—even though a few others and I could run circles around some of those dirtbags. It wasn't quite the life for me. Chief Lewis didn't have any hard feelings about my resignation, and he'd even suggested I become a private detective instead. The rest was history, and I'd never looked back.

Even now, that shiny silver badge still came in handy, especially when I needed to trip up a suspect. But having it around could get me in big trouble. Chief Lewis pulled the strings to make sure that didn't happen. As a private dick, I solved smaller cases and did the dirty work so the rookie cops could swoop in like vultures and take all the credit. But I didn't mind. I was getting paid, and Chief Lewis had a good eye on me and knew that I was a-okay. In a way, I still had one foot in the force, having a great contact like him only a phone call away.

I turned off the radiator under the window and went to the coatrack by the front door. I shrugged on my brown leather trench coat over my black turtleneck and denim bell-bottoms. After putting on my gloves and placing the rest of the items in their respective pockets, I plucked my dark-green fedora from the rack and slipped it on. My thick, curly hair spilled out from it like a lion's mane.

Leaving the office, I jiggled my key into a set of three locks that secured the door from the outside. It wouldn't take much for a determined robber to break them, but the locks were enough to add a bit of annoyance, at least. Not like they would find anything they would consider valuable in my office, anyway, unless they had a particular penchant for Dick Tracy comics. But I pitied the fool who laid their grubby hands on my coveted reading material, because no god would save them from the wrath of an angry Tootsie Carter.

CHAPTER 2

The ride to Marlene's Diner took almost an hour by bus, as it stopped at practically every stop along the way to pick up or drop off passengers. I was lucky to find an empty space on the bench seat tucked safely into one of the back corners of the bus. I'd always preferred having my back to the wall, where I could get a good look at everyone coming and going, a leftover habit from my old days on the force.

The bus was beginning to empty, and I was one stop away from my destination, when the bus pulled over to the corner of East 168th Street and Third Avenue. I halted reviewing my case notes and looked up from my notebook. Two men wearing Wall

Street–wannabe suits and carrying black briefcases boarded and made their way to the back. I pegged them as either salesmen or insurance agents of the sleazy variety, from the way they strutted along like they carried gold in their pockets. But I'd dealt with their types enough times to know that it was all a façade, and they almost never had a pot to piss in.

They both looked like they'd had another long day of poor sales or they were inundated with insurance claims—most likely theft or arson—that were probably stacked higher than the Empire State Building. These days, it was bad news all around for businesses, especially when the country was barely surviving last year's stock market crash. Wall Street was a zoo right now. And here I thought being a private dick was stressful.

One of them, an older Hispanic man, eyed an empty space beside me on the bench, gave me a curious once-over with his calculating hazel eyes, and quietly sat. I looked sideways at him, noting the briefcase he had in his lap. It bore an emblem of a lightning bolt on the front and "Insta-surance— Insurance in a Flash!" beneath it. *Wow, I'm good*, I thought.

Faint wrinkles traced the man's ruddy, weathered face and around his neatly trimmed salt-and-pepper facial hair. The pungent odor of tobacco wafted from him.

His companion, a clean-shaven Black gentleman, wore thick glasses. When he looked my way, his eyebrows rose. He nodded, smiling crookedly. "Hey, sweet thing. Whatcha doing back here all by yourself? Want some company?"

I simply gave him a brief, expressionless stare then returned to my case notes. I watched him out of the corner of my eye. He seemed like a smart one to take my quiet, yet obvious hint, as he cleared his throat and lowered himself in the seat next to his older companion. I was no stranger to the looks, catcalls, and whistles from desperate turkeys looking for a quick shag. And I knew they were desperate, because I was worlds apart from looking like a *Playboy* model. At least, I thought so. I owned exactly one skirt, one pair of heels, and one dress, all of them Christmas gifts from my mother, and all of them worn only on those ultra-rare occasions that required me to "be a lady." Dresses and heels tended to get in the way of my work, especially when I had to chase a suspect. Or fight for my life.

I was in no hurry to settle down, not when there was so much more excitement to be had in this detective life. Navigating in a man's world was only half the fun.

The older man looked sideways at me and let out an airy chuckle. He murmured to his friend, "You're losing your touch, Joe."

As the bus sputtered off again, Joe blew a raspberry. "Man, that chick don't know what she's missin'."

I held my tongue, refraining from letting out some choice words. I decided to "be a lady" tonight.

"*Ella parece tiene sus cosas en orden,*" the older man muttered to himself. He reached into the inner breast pocket of his suit and pulled out a pack of cigarettes. He slid one out and rolled it around in his fingers a moment. "In any event," he said to Joe, "I'm putting my neck on the line tonight. Two hundred on Wesson." He stuck the cigarette in his mouth, pulled out a silver Insta-surance-engraved lighter from his other pocket, and lit it.

Joe snorted. "I'm tellin' you, man, Wesson's gonna have his hands full."

"Doubtful. His opponent is a washed-up has-been."

Sighing, I slipped on my gloves, then I reached up with two fingers and tugged on the yellow pull-cord draped across the window to request my next stop. Most sports talk tended to go right out my other ear, unless it pertained to baseball, and even then, my mind was always elsewhere with cases. I barely found time to keep up with the latest news.

Around eight thirty, the bus pulled up to the East 168th Street and Park Avenue stop. I got off, along with a few other passengers, and walked a quarter mile the rest of the way to Webster Avenue. A light gust of gritty, chilly air stung my cheeks and the tip of my nose. Lousy springtime weather, this was. It had to be close to thirty degrees, and the forecast promised steadily falling temperatures as the night drew on. I tipped my hat down farther and stuffed my hands into my trench coat pockets.

Marlene's Diner sat midway down the wide street, across from one of the towering Webster projects. First opened in '61, the diner was primarily frequented by off-duty cops and legal suits en route to Grand Concourse. I'd come here once or twice with my parents for a quick lunch, way back in my youth. The diner's fish-and-chips house special was out of this world, and they were the only ones around who made those killer Tootsie Roll milkshakes. I didn't know why I hadn't come here more often, then or now. Then, I guessed, my parents—especially my dad—had been the frugal types, and eating out was a rare, luxurious treat. Nowadays, my stomach would probably eat itself by the time I braved the cross-town traffic to make my way all the way over here.

It was 8:45 p.m. when I reached the diner's entrance. A welcoming warmth from the hot stoves, coffee pots, and the nearby radiator soothed my face, thawing out the bitter chill from my skin. I inhaled the familiar mouth-watering aroma of the house special, and I had to remind myself why I needed to make this stop brief. I raised the brim of my hat slightly and observed the diner's patrons. Long-faced blue-collar workers occupied the booths. Chatty college kids had claimed most of the chrome-trimmed swivel stools at the lunch counter. A lone busboy traversed the opposite end of the diner, sweeping the grimy, green-and-white checkered floor, while a waitress zipped to and from each of the booths like an excited, sugar-infused ant. Another waitress stood behind a register at the lunch counter, cashing out a waiting patron. A plate of piping-hot fish-and-chips appeared at the small serving window beneath a metal order wheel clipped with food orders written on white, notecard-sized slips. Beyond the window, I also caught a glimpse of two busy cooks scrambling about the kitchen. Propped up on a shelf next to the lunch counter was an old radio, hissing out the staticky sounds of Motown's latest hit.

Tugging off my gloves, I approached the lunch counter. The cashier sorted a stack of bills in the cash drawer then speared a handwritten guest check through a metal paper spindle with a stack of others. Despite her appearing much older, I pegged the woman to be somewhere in her late forties. Permanent frown lines marred her sweat-slicked forehead and around her mouth. Tiny white strands of hair streaked the edges of her thick, puffy bun. As she looked at me, the lines in her forehead became more prominent, and a score of crow's feet appeared around her narrowing dark-brown eyes. "Yeah? What can I do for you, sweetie?"

I leaned against the counter, giving the nearby unsuspecting college kids another quick once-over before turning back to the cashier. A white nametag that read "Nat" hung crookedly over the left breast of her teal food-stained uniform. "Evening. I'm looking for the manager."

She scanned me up and down with an arched eyebrow. "That'd be me. Can I help you?"

"My name is Detective Carter. Does a woman by the name of Luanda Miles work here?"

Nat's eyes widened, and the crow's feet disappeared. "D-Detective? As in the police? You got a badge?"

"Yup." I flashed my old police badge just long enough for her to see that it was the real deal but not long enough for her to read the fine print.

She swallowed once then leaned in closer, and her voice became a low mutter. "Yeah, Lu works here. What's going on? Is… Is she all right?"

I matched her volume. "Not sure. I need to find her first. She's apparently been missing since Monday."

Her shoulders slumped, and a look of pain washed over her sienna-toned face. "I haven't seen Lu since Friday. I only work here two days a week, usually the first shift, but sometimes the second— like today."

I fished through one of the inner pockets of my trench coat and pulled out my notebook. After unhooking the pen from the spirals, I turned to a fresh page and jotted some notes. "Noticed anything different about her last Friday?"

Nat shrugged and shook her head. "Nah, she's usually hanging around those other girls, Cheryl and Theresa, gossiping. Lu's a sweet little thing, though. Has a way with the customers—the men, especially—and gets the most tips."

I arched an eyebrow. "What kind of 'way' are we talking here?"

"Have you seen her? I don't know why she ain't on the cover of *Vogue*."

"That fine, huh?"

Nat chuckled. "Honey, you just don't know."

Maybe Lu is related to Pam Grier. Distant cousin, perhaps? "Well, I do know her husband is worried sick at home."

"I would be, too, if I were him. He married himself one foxy mama, I'll tell you what." She retrieved a cleaning rag and an unmarked spray bottle from beneath the register, then she spritzed the top of the counter. The lemon-scented cleaner wafted through the air as she wiped the harvest-gold laminate in slow circles.

"You get a lot of male customers here looking for her?" I asked.

"Well, you know. We get the regulars—the few who've come here enough times to learn her schedule." She didn't look up from her cleaning.

I scanned the diner, trying to pick out some potential admirers. "Any of them here now?"

"Don't look like it. Lu ain't on the schedule today."

"You know the names of any of her admirers?"

Nat chuckled. "Harris, Trey, and Jack are three I know for sure, because they give the biggest tips. Don't know their last names, though."

I wrote down the names, though I wasn't sure how much good this would do me. "Do you know if any of the other employees have seen her lately?"

"Maybe one of the cooks, but..." Nat nodded toward the waitress serving coffee to two men in a booth. "Theresa over there, probably. She and Lu often work the same shift."

"Swell. I'll have a little talk with her."

"We're closing in thirty minutes. Mind hanging out till then before you start grilling her with questions? We've been short-staffed tonight. She and I are the only ones working the floor."

I really did mind staying longer than I should, because my stomach was growling after I'd spotted a plate of a piping-hot, juicy steak being slid into the serving window. And it took every ounce of my willpower to refrain from ordering a Tootsie Roll milkshake. *No. Work first. Then food.*

"Fine," I conceded, then an idea suddenly came to me, which graciously hauled away my spur-of-the-moment appetite. "Say, is there a place where the employees keep their things?"

"Yeah, there are a couple of filing cabinets in the back." Nat thumbed toward a nearby steel swinging door marked Employees Only. "Lu uses the drawer marked *B*."

"Mind if I take a look?"

"Well, I guess I ain't really have a choice now, huh? I mean, that poor girl's missing and all. Go on, check it out, Detective."

"Appreciate your cooperation."

"I just hope you find her soon."

I headed for the Employees Only door as another patron approached the counter. I slipped through the door, which opened up to a tiny, narrow passage. The powerful, mouthwatering aroma of seasoned fried perch wafted from another swinging door to the right, which led to the kitchen. Through the door's circular window, I noticed the two cooks continuing to work the stove and prep area tirelessly.

At the end of the hallway, I reached a room lit by a single low-hanging lightbulb attached to the popcorn ceiling. The room appeared slightly bigger than my sardine-can-sized bedroom. Two metal folding chairs and a card table were arranged against one wall, a couple of magazines stacked under one of the table's uneven legs. Two filing cabinets stood up against the opposite wall.

I tugged open Drawer B. It was fairly clean inside, save for a wadded gum wrapper and a neatly folded black half-apron. I checked the apron and discovered a blank guest check pad in one of its pockets. *Nothing unusual here...*

Frowning, I thumbed idly through the blank pages of the pad from cover to cover like a flipbook. I was about to return the pad, then my fingers rubbed over something on the back cover. I turned it over. Some indented writing was barely visible. I held it up closer to the hanging lightbulb and tilted it slightly. The writing appeared to be an address to someplace in Queens. Beneath the address also read: *W - 10:30p.*

'*W...*' *Wednesday?* I wondered. Tonight was Wednesday. I had no idea *which* Wednesday the note meant, but it might be worth checking out. Lu hadn't been seen since Monday, so she could've written it much earlier. I transcribed the info into my notebook and slid the pad back into the apron's pocket. Wherever the address led, it was the only clue I had for now.

The caged wall clock over the doorway read a quarter after nine. If I could squeeze a few answers out of Miss Theresa, I would have enough time to grab a taxi and book it to Queens in under an hour.

I returned to the main dining area. The place had emptied out, with only a couple of the college students lingering at the lunch counter. But even they appeared to be wrapping up their conversation and preparing to leave. The neon Open sign was shut off, as was the radio. The hiss of running water and clinking dishes echoed from the kitchen. Nat was going through the stack of guest checks, seemingly unaware of my presence, while Theresa went around to the booths, wiping them down and clearing away stray dishes. The busboy brushed past me, wheeling his steel bucket behind him, and disappeared through the swinging door. I approached Theresa and stood in her path before she could work on the next booth. She halted and looked up at me with a start.

"Excuse me," I said. "Theresa, was it?"

She swallowed and gave a small nod. "Y-Yeah? Who are—"

"Detective Carter." I flashed my badge. "I'm investigating Luanda Miles's disappearance."

Her eyes widened, and her mouth opened slightly. "Lu's gone? You... You sure?"

I looked at her curiously, taking a mental picture of her smooth chestnut face, noting the nervousness in her dark-brown eyes and the subtle twitch of her left eyelid. "Well, she's apparently been missing since Monday. You have time to answer a few questions?" I gestured to the empty booth.

She swallowed again and nodded. "Yeah, I guess..."

We plunked down in the stiff booth seats, and I watched her from across the table. If she had something to share, I intended to pull it out of her. "First of all, chill out. You're not in trouble. I just need some answers."

"Sorry, I-I just can't believe Lu's missing."

"I can get to the bottom of this if you cooperate. Can you dig it?"

She nodded again and moistened her lips.

I opened my notebook. "So, you and Luanda are friends?"

"We're just coworkers. We talk here and there but nothing really more than that." Her eyelids fluttered downward, and she drew small circles on the laminate with her finger.

I reached over, placed my hand over her fidgety one, and held it firmly in place. "Mind looking at me and saying that again?"

Her jaw clenched, and she lifted her gaze. "We're coworkers. We talk sometimes. That's all."

I removed my hand. "What do you guys talk about?"

She gave a light shrug. "Shopping, television shows, music, weekend plans, latest gossip..."

"Men?" I suggested with raised eyebrows.

Theresa snorted. "No, Cheryl's the one who talks about men. She's the only one of us who's still single, after all."

"Does Luanda ever talk to Cheryl?"

"Sometimes, yeah. And wouldn't you know, Cheryl was supposed to work tonight, but she called in sick." She frowned and averted her gaze again. "I called her today before I came in to work, but she didn't pick up. I dunno. Something's not right. Cheryl seemed fine when I saw her yesterday."

"You talked to Cheryl yesterday?"

She nodded. "We went shopping."

"So, what do you suspect is up with her?"

Theresa sighed and looked back at me. "Don't get me wrong. I love Cheryl like a sister, but she's such an instigator. She knows damned well Lu's a married woman, but Cheryl's playing around, trying to get her in trouble with the way Lu turns heads. Maybe she's just using Lu in order to snag herself a man. I dunno."

I arched an eyebrow. "How would she do that?"

"Lu pretty much has the men wrapped around her finger. Lu acts naïve to it, but Cheryl knows what's up. I'm sure she'd use her friend's superpowers to her own advantage."

"Pretty crummy way to treat a so-called friend."

Theresa shrugged. "That's just how Cheryl is sometimes, especially when it comes to relationships."

"So, you think Luanda might be messing around with another man?"

"I don't think so. I mean, as flirty as she can be, she seems pretty faithful to her husband, Greg. All she's been talking about lately is how excited she was for their upcoming anniversary. She's been working extra hours to help pay for a cruise to Bermuda."

"So I've heard." I glanced over my fresh page of notes and rubbed my chin. "Has anyone come here recently that's gotten a little extra sweet on Luanda?"

She tapped her finger against her lips and looked thoughtful for a moment. "Well, not Lu, but... There was this one guy who came in last month. Pretty fine piece of work. A jock. I think his name was Darin. Anyway, he was polite to Lu and was extra sweet on Cheryl. Pretty soon, Cheryl and Lu were going off with Darin most weeknights."

"Where did they go?"

She wrinkled her nose. "Some gym. I don't know exactly where."

"You have a name?"

"I don't remember."

I rolled my eyes. "Swell. So what were they all doing there?"

"Cheryl said they were watching him train and lift weights. But I think it was more like ogling his muscles—at least Cheryl probably was, anyway. It seemed like every time I saw her, the first thing she had to talk about was how many more pounds he'd lifted."

"Cheryl and Lu never invited you along?"

"They did, but I didn't want to go. I'm not into that kind of thing. Besides…" She held up her left hand, revealing her wedding band. "I got me a good man already."

"Sounds like I'll need to pay Cheryl a visit. What's her last name, by the way?"

"Ross."

"You got her address?"

Theresa nodded and rapped it out, though with some hesitation. Cheryl lived in Soundview, in an apartment complex that overlooked the Bronx River, not far from my place. After I took the information down in my notebook, I said, "If you want Luanda found, then do *not* call Cheryl and warn her I'm coming to see her."

She chewed her bottom lip. "I won't, Detective. I promise."

"All right." I scooted out of the booth. "That's all the questions I have for now."

"Will you let me know if you find out something?" She looked at me with hopeful eyes.

"I'll be in touch. Give me your info."

She wasn't as hesitant to give out her telephone number and address, which was in Morris Heights. I scribbled down the info then asked, "By the way, do you know what this address belongs to?" I showed her the address I'd copied from Luanda's drawer.

Theresa's face scrunched as she scrutinized it, then she shook her head. "Doesn't look familiar. But I don't go to Queens all too often."

I tucked my notebook away and put my gloves back on. "Thanks. You've been helpful." I wrapped my trench coat around my body, tilted my hat downward, and stepped back out into the bitter cold of night. My next stop would be the address from Lu's locker. With less than twenty minutes to spare before ten thirty, I hailed a taxi and decided to test my luck in the unknown reaches of Queens.

CHAPTER 3

I usually visited Queens for cases or, during those rare occasions I had time to kill, to see old friends. Unfortunately, this wasn't going to be one of those nights when I could drop in for a reunion. As for the case, however, Lady Luck was on my side. I ended up with a Checker cabby who knew his way around the boroughs like the back of his hand.

Sid Bonado was his name. At forty-nine years old, he was a Brooklyn-bred, Italian-American war veteran and former welterweight Golden Gloves boxer. During our twenty-minute trip, Sid told me stories of his boxing glory days, as well as recent, grim stories of faces he'd bashed and bones he'd broken when robbers tried to jack him, usually, at gunpoint. I knew he wasn't jive talking. He'd grown up during a time when honest, hard work and keeping customers happy meant something. His stories were the real deal, all right, and he didn't feel sorry for all the fools who'd tried to rough him up. I didn't feel sorry for them either. I couldn't remember the last time I'd felt safe in this city. He'd earned enough of my respect that I threw him my name. I was willing to bet he would make a perfect doorman for our frequently robbed building too. *I should introduce him to Sam sometime.*

"Here we are, li'l lady," Sid announced in his gruff, bulldog tone.

We were parked along the garbage-strewn curb of a narrow one-way street in front of a rundown auto shop. The amber glow of a nearby streetlight illuminated the Closed sign that hung in the shop's security-barred window, and the graffiti-covered metal garage door was rolled down. I scrunched my nose. *Why would Luanda come here?*

I wasn't too sure about her husband's finances, but I couldn't imagine her being able to afford her own car on a waitress's part-time paycheck. Then again, she apparently did get lots of tips. A cynical thought crossed my mind. *Maybe Lu snagged herself a sugar daddy.*

That was ridiculous. Maybe. This address could've meant anything or nothing at all. Or maybe the five was actually a three. I sighed. I'd hit a dead end already. *Guess it's time to see Cheryl.*

"You okay?" Sid's gaze lingered on me from the rearview mirror.

"Yeah…" There seemed to be nothing else in this dark, seedy-looking area, other than a large, weather-worn brick building across the street. The building's bright neon sign displayed the words "Sunnyside Garden." The lighted marquee below it read:

BINGO - MON FRI
AMT FGHT NGHT - WED

Small groups of people bundled up in coats and hats were hanging out in front of the building. Dim light seeped from the building's tall bay windows, as an event was currently taking place inside.

"You know, all the times I've been to Queens, I've never been in this area," I said absently, watching two suited men enter the building.

Sid guffawed. "Ya jokin', doll! This is where it all goes down, right 'ere." He stuck his thumb toward the building. "My ol' stomping grounds. Fought there in the amateur bouts back in '51—"

Anticipating another boxing war story about to happen, I held up my finger. "Um, is that meter sill running?"

He glanced at the meter then back at me. "Not no more, it ain't." He slapped his hand over the meter flag, and the machine ceased its steady ticking at $4.25. "Y'know somethin', Ms. Carter? You're all right. Like a breath of fresh air in this clogged-up town."

"Thanks, I think…"

"So, where was I?"

"Your old stomping grounds, back in '51."

He cracked a smile. "Oh yeah. I remember this one night. Thursday. Undercard match right before the main event. Had to fight this big, mean son of a bitch named Palooka Pat. He was light on his feet but had a glass jaw. So in round three, I let 'im have it. *Bam!*" He smacked his fist in his hand. "He ain't never seen more stars before in his life, I'll tell ya what."

I smirked. "I would've loved to see that."

"Eh… well, you won't see that no more from me. Busted up my knee pretty bad one day, and that was the end of my career. Hung up the gloves nineteen years ago. These days, I just slug the punks who think I'm some washed-up old man."

"Trust me, Sid. I think you're the meanest, toughest cat I've met in a long time."

He grinned. "Thanks, doll. You dig boxing?"

"Eh, it's all right. Watching it long enough makes me wanna crack some skulls."

"Haha. I know whatcha mean. All that fierce, high energy gets your adrenaline pumpin'."

"I caught part of the big Foreman-Ali fight last year. But that was only because it was on the television at my friend's bar—and practically every bar in the city. Pretty entertaining. I like the way Ali moves."

Sid laughed. "He ain't called the Greatest for nothin'. Anyway, you should go watch a couple fights in there. They've been doing amateur boxing night every Wednesday for a couple months now. Small-time gig compared to the ones on Saturdays, though. These are the nights when all the up-'n-comin' talent try to make a name." His pockmarked face suddenly brightened. "Oh, hey, I forgot. Tonight, there're supposed to be a couple o' good headliners."

"Ali's fighting?" I joked.

"Nah." He picked up the folded sports section of a newspaper from the front passenger's seat. "Here it is. I was readin' about it this morning. First fight is former featherweight champ Darin Rivers from Philly versus Brooklyn's own current champ, Shawn Wesson. Second fight is former light heavyweight champ Zion Malone from Patterson versus the current champ, Pete Sanders, a kid from Boston."

"Eh, sounds interesting, but..." I perked up. *Darin. Wesson. Wait a minute...* "Say, mind if I see that paper?"

"Sure thing, doll." He slid the paper between the gaps of the bulletproof partition.

I examined the quarter-page article. *Is this the same Darin that Theresa mentioned?* I ran my finger down to the end of the article, where the time and venue were mentioned: "Undercard matches begin at 6p. First main event starts at 10:30p."

I looked back at the arena. A large lighted clock hanging above the entrance read 10:35 p.m. My women's intuition—practically the only female thing I never turned off—was telling me that I might be on a trail again. "Y'know, on second thought," I said, returning the paper to him, "I think I *will* watch a few fights tonight."

"That's swell. Betcha won't be disappointed none either." He chuckled.

Grinning, I pulled out a ten-dollar bill and slipped it through the partition. "Should be exciting. Keep the change."

He whistled, his eyes lighting up brighter than Christmas, then he awkwardly adjusted his brown wool flat-cap. "Damn! Ya sure are a-okay in my book, lady."

"Trust me, you've more than earned that tip."

He opened the glove compartment, grabbed a brown business card, then handed it to me. "You ever need to go someplace else, I'm your man to take ya there."

I stuck the card in my coat pocket and opened the door. "Right on. I'll give you a ring soon enough. Don't worry. Later, Sid."

I got out of the car and crossed the street, glancing over my shoulder just in time to watch the yellow cab speed off. I brushed past a bundled-up couple standing on the sidewalk at a bus stop, enjoying a cigarette, then hurried through the entrance door, where a poster was plastered on one of its windows, advertising tonight's event. In the dimly lit vestibule, I stopped at the box office window to slide my five-dollar entrance fee through the iron bars to the attendant then continued down the corridor. Its walls were decorated with tattered remnants of old posters and flyers that were long since ripped away from their adhesives. At the end of the hallway, past the entrance to the bar and lounge, an attendant stood outside a set of double doors. The sounds of a roaring crowd intensified as I approached. When one of the doors swung open, the crowd's sounds blared louder, and a man in a suit and bright-red tie exited. His curious blue eyes scanned me briefly as we passed each other, and when I turned my head slightly to view him out of the corner of my eye, I could still feel his gaze. Finally, his head turned back around, and he continued toward the vestibule. *Do I know him?*

After the attendant tore off one end of my ticket, I entered a dark, smoke-filled arena surrounded by a score of wood-topped bleachers, as well as a row of wooden chairs in the ringside seating area. Humid, musty, air of cigarettes, cigars, and sweat smacked my senses, as if I'd stepped into some tiny hole-in-the-wall gym. The place looked about as big as a high-school gymnasium, but even the lively, predominantly male crowd that occupied most of the bleachers and chairs made the place seem larger than it was.

The two headliners were already bobbing and feinting in the blue-canvassed boxing ring, feeling each other out, spotlighted by the hazy light from the arena's ceiling fixtures. Red-white-and-blue bunting draped along the walls of the arena created a festive touch amid the otherwise-tense atmosphere. Men in expensive suits filled the ringside seats. I found an empty spot at the end of one of the bleachers, not far behind a row of wooden chairs, where I could exit quickly without wading through a sea of spectators.

A few of the high rollers perched on the edges of their seats, but most of them sat back and stayed cool as they enjoyed their expensive smokes. Meanwhile, the regular folks in the bleachers were on their feet, shouting and pumping their fists like they were out for blood as they cheered on the two contenders.

I wondered if Luanda and Cheryl were here tonight. It was difficult to make out faces in the crowd, especially the ones sitting higher up in the bleachers.

As if feeding off the crowd's roar, the two sweat-drenched young men in the ring dropped their caution and went at it. A lone balding referee wearing a white button-down shirt, brown plaid pants, and a matching bow tie sidled around the two fighters, watching them intensely. One of the fighters, a man wearing green trunks with white trim, jabbed at his slightly taller opponent, who was in blue trunks with red trim. Blue Trunks bobbed and weaved deftly, then he countered with a left hook. I had no idea which one was Darin. Both looked like healthy, strong men who spent the majority of their days in the gym. The match was obviously still in the early rounds, because both of their attractive, clean-shaven mugs were pretty much untouched.

The bleachers and floor vibrated as nearby spectators stomped furiously in a rhythm that thundered off the walls. The energy in this place made my heart pound. The feeling was much more intense than what I felt while watching a boxing match on television.

"He's open! He's open! C'mon, Wes! Get 'im! Get 'im!" shouted a middle-aged man beside me. He was dressed twenty years too young and sported a brown shag haircut that matched his ugly brown striped bell-bottoms. He focused on the fight. With fire in his eyes, fists raised closed to his face, he made small jabs and uppercuts in the air as if puppeteering the fighters' bodies. I was tempted to ask the dude which contender was which, but he looked like he would chew my head off if my interference made him miss a second of the fight. So I remained in my seat, looking on, trying to take my best guess.

"To the side! To the side! Right here! Rib shot!" the man shouted.

I leaned forward and focused hard. Blue Trunks held his hands a little high, creating a small opening just below his elbow. As quickly as I spotted it, however, he lowered his arms.

The man beside me hissed out a string of curses. "Damn it, Wes! That was your shot, man!" He stomped the floor and shook his fist.

Right. So Blue Trunks must be Darin.

The bell suddenly rang, signaling the end of the round. The referee pulled the fighters apart and sent them off to their respective sides, where cornermen swarmed them. The man beside me plopped down in his seat, grumbling more curses as he glared ahead. The suited men who sat ringside began chatting with one another, pointing toward the ring while they casually tipped ash from their cigars and cigarettes.

One of the men in Darin's corner, a burly cat with a white towel draped over his shoulders, stood in front of Darin, balled his fists, and shook them as he spoke to him. Meanwhile, another man drenched Darin's face and mouth with water from a bottle, and a cut man applied some sort of salve on Darin's cheek. Darin gave Towel Guy a small hand gesture. The big man deflated then made his way out of the ring.

A blond ring girl wearing a barely there halter top, a pair of short-shorts that showed off her mile-long legs, and black four-inch heels sashayed once around the ring, holding up a large Round 4 sign, then exited down a small set of steps.

The fighters returned from their corners and faced off again. I didn't take my eyes off Darin. Something about the way he moved seemed strange. He danced around the ring, sometimes lowering his hands for a split second, only to raise them again before his opponent could attack. Darin was playing with him, like a lion played with its food. Boos poured from the unimpressed crowd.

"Don't take that from him!" the man beside me yelled.

Clearly, most of these cats had their money on Shawn Wesson. I continued watching the unfavored fighter carefully. His dark eyes seemed focused somewhere outside the ring most of the time, except when he needed to block an incoming blow from his opponent. Perhaps he didn't consider the guy a threat. Occasionally, his gaze flitted toward the ringside seating area. The moment I saw the whites of his eyes as he glanced into the executive crowd, I sensed a spark of fear. *Did he see someone he knows? Luanda, maybe?* I wondered.

I rose slowly from my chair, craning my neck to peer at the group. There were only a few women among them, and none of them came close to Pam Grier quality. And all of them sat awfully close to their men, like perfect arm candy.

Shawn let loose a fast, straight punch toward Darin's face and connected. Darin's head barely snapped back. The boos suddenly lessened, and cheers ensued.

"Yeah! Yeah! That's the way!" my excited bleacher-mate yelled, pumping his fist.

Shawn punched him again and again, landing every hit at Darin's face and body. Darin hardly flinched, and he didn't even try to counter, even though Shawn looked like he was giving him everything he had. *Is Darin giving those to him?*

"C'mon, Wesson! Ten more seconds! Ya got 'im! Ya got 'im!"

The bleacher crowd's cheering intensified. Even some of the suits rose to their feet.

Darin took another blow to the jaw. His head whipped to the side. He paused, his gaze flitting to the audience again before his focus returned to Shawn. Darin made a few quick shuffles then countered with a lightning-fast left-uppercut that sent Shawn reeling backward, a shower of sweat flinging off his face. Shawn teetered then collapsed to the ground.

The referee steadily counted to ten. Shawn made a feeble attempt to sit up, only to flop back down on the mat again. As the tenth count was announced, the bell rang, and the arena went into an uproar.

The referee waved his hands, signaling that the match was over, and he grabbed Darin's arm and yanked it up in the air in victory.

"Winner by knockout and new featherweight champion is Darin Rivers!" an announcer's voice blared from the overhead speakers.

Well, that was… interesting.

The tension in the air grew fiercer, as the entire place erupted into chaos. My exasperated bench-mate swore as he ran his hands through his mop of hair. Some of the bleacher crowd flipped the bird toward center ring, while others tossed wads of paper and garbage. In a fit of rage as several ringside chairs were shoved back, many of the suited men stood, blocking my view of the ring. I spotted the two men I'd ridden the bus with earlier, as they followed a group of people storming out of the arena. Near the exit, a commotion suddenly broke out among as several men got shoved aside, then another man pointed toward a blur of a shadow that zipped through the door.

My bench-mate headed toward the exit, and I followed. As the crowd of furious spectators thinned, I looked back toward center ring. The referee watched Shawn's cornermen drag him off. Meanwhile, Darin's water boy and cut man looked around, confused, like they'd lost something. Apparently, they had, because Darin was gone.

CHAPTER 4

The vestibule in Sunnyside Arena was a crowded madhouse of disgruntled people ranting over the Rivers-Wesson upset as though they'd lost their entire life savings. Instead of sticking around to eavesdrop on the complaints, I trailed two suited men. The Black guy, who walked with a slight limp, wore a brown plaid jacket and a matching brown fedora. The other, an olive-skinned Italian, was hatless and wore a powder-blue jacket. Both rushed down a narrow side hallway beside the arena's inner entrance toward a dark stairwell. I didn't recognize the men, but by the way they hightailed it like two racehorses, I figured they would lead me right to the runaway boxer, Darin Rivers. In the midst of the post-fight chaos, Darin had managed to disappear in plain sight among the crowd.

When the two men were footsteps away from the stairwell, I slipped into an alcove in front of a closed janitor's closet. I peeked around the corner at Mr. Powder-Blue and Mr. Brown, who warily glanced about as they conversed in hushed tones. Moments later, they rushed down the stairs. I waited a few beats in case they had any friends coming, but I only heard the echo of the vestibule chaos. Leaving my hiding spot, I hustled to the shallow staircase and peered into the dimly lit sub-level. A sign painted on the concrete wall on the stairwell read Locker Rooms/Changing Area, with an arrow pointing down. A discarded flyer advertising tonight's fight lay by the stairs.

An idea suddenly sprung into my mind, and I swiped up the paper then pulled my notebook from my coat pocket. After another quick check over my shoulder for anyone else heading this way, I trod silently down the stairs and emerged into another narrow block-wall corridor. The stale air carried a mildewy odor. The muffled chatter and tromping of the vestibule crowd above gently shook the chains of the hanging fluorescent lights.

Thunderous pounding echoed from the left. A man's voice barked, "Get your ass outta there!"

The two men I'd followed stood at the far end of the hallway. I slinked closer, the soles of my boots padding along the concrete floor more quietly than a cat's paws. Their backs turned, the men stood in front of a door to one of the locker rooms. They were seemingly unaware of my presence, and I preferred it that way. More time for me to figure out what business they had with Darin.

Light reflected off a fat silver watch that Mr. Powder-Blue wore on his left wrist as he pounded on the closed door. "Open this fucking door! Now!"

They waited a moment, but there was no answer. Mr. Brown nervously adjusted the sleeves of his coat and turned to his friend. "He ain't comin' out, Curt."

Mr. Powder-Blue shoved him aside. "He better come out. I want my damn money." Growling, he kicked and pounded on the door again. "You hear me, you two-timing son of a bitch? You won't be breathing when I get done with you! And your girlfriend's good as dead!"

Mr. Brown backed away from the door. "He ain't listening, man."

"Oh, he will." Curt turned to his partner. "Call Vick. Tell 'im to get ready to smoke the broad."

I widened my eyes. *They're gonna...*

Mr. Brown spun on his heel, hustled in my direction, then halted. Regaining my composure, I continued walking toward him, passing under a buzzing fluorescent light, and flashed a giddy smile. He looked like someone who would talk or at least give me a clue or two. I just had to ask the right questions and push the right buttons.

The fear on Mr. Brown's face disappeared, replaced by a rigid, calculating expression. He approached me with deliberate steps. "Who are you?"

My plastered smile stretched. "Hi! I just wanted to get Mr. Rivers's autograph after that *dynamite* performance tonight," I said in a bubbly tone, holding up my notebook and flyer. "I tried to catch him, but he was gone."

He scowled. "He ain't down here."

I furrowed my brow. "What do you mean 'he ain't down here'? I'm pretty sure I saw him come this way."

"You saw wrong." He flicked his wrist, making a shooing gesture at me. "Now scram, baby."

Baby… I held my tongue to prevent a few choice words from flinging out. "Look, he's gotta be down here. I checked the other locker room down the hallway. C'mon, let me just see him for a minute. I just want his autograph—and maybe his towel—or better yet, his glove. Oh, to hold that same sweaty glove he used to knock out Shawn Wesson!"

"No!"

I flinched. "Well, y'don't have to get all bent outta shape about it."

"Who the hell are you talking to, Mel?" Curt called, abandoning the door and joining his friend. He looked me up and down, then a crease formed between his thick, dark eyebrows. "Who's this broad?"

"I'm Darin Rivers's number-one fan, and I want his autograph. He is so strong and dreamy, and watching the way he just knocked out the champ makes me want to swoon!" I rambled. "I really, really, *really* need his autograph!"

"I told her he ain't here," Mel muttered to his friend, who rolled his eyes.

My gaze bounced between the two men then widened. "Wait a minute. A-Are you guys his *managers* or something? You hiding him from me? I'm a long-time fan, and I've waited ages for this moment to finally get his autograph and meet him face-to-face."

Curt cleared his throat. "Ah, yeah. That's right. I'm his manager."

I widened my eyes larger than saucers. "Really? Swell! So that means you can introduce me to him! Mr. Rivers is here, right?"

"Yeah, but he had a rough night. He's not talking to any fans right now. Catch him another time."

I wrinkled my nose. "What d'ya mean 'he's had a rough night'? He just beat Shawn Wesson, the featherweight champ!"

His jaw clenched. "He did, but sometimes victories come with a price. You follow? Now get outta here."

"But—!"

"Beat it, before I call security."

Victories come with a price, eh? I lifted my head, giving them both a dubious look. I'd never heard of a manager being furious at his client for winning—if this guy was even his manager. They were up to something, all right.

"Fine." I did an about-face and headed for the stairs. I turned my head slightly, keeping the two in my peripheral vision. They didn't take their eyes off me. I turned and began ascending the stairwell. When I was halfway up, I stomped repeatedly then transitioned to slow, quieter steps. Afterward, I hugged the wall, bracing myself on the banister, and crept up the stairs, keeping my footsteps silent.

"What if that broad comes back down here looking for him?" I heard Mel mutter.

"She won't," Curt assured. "Now, hurry up and make that call. I'm gonna find a way to get that door open."

I took another silent step up.

Mel grunted. The sound of footsteps approached the stairwell. I continued upward quietly, and with only four more steps to go before I reached the top, I glanced behind me. Mel's shadow loomed near the base of stairwell. The footfalls stopped, and his shadow spun around.

"Hey, Curt…" he said, his voice slightly above a whisper.

"Go!" Curt snapped.

"What if Darin ain't even in there?"

"Look, there's only one way in and out of that room, and it's through that door. He's in there. Now, quit stalling and get your ass upstairs!"

Mel's shadow jumped, then he hastened toward the stairwell. With only two more steps to go, I white-knuckled the banister and braced myself to climb both steps at once. The banister let out an echoing creak when I put too much weight on it. I raced out of the stairwell entrance and rounded a corner as Mel yelled, "Hey!"

I hustled down the hallway toward the vestibule, not looking back. The angry crowd had thinned, and the place was trashed with torn ticket stubs, flyers, and other garbage. A group of four suited men stood near the public wall telephone by the entrance. I recognized one of the men—I'd passed the one chatting on the telephone when I first arrived. There was no mistaking the hard look in his eyes or that bright-red tie that would make a bull go into a frenzy.

I slowed my run to long, quick strides as I headed toward the exit doors, casting a final glance at the crowd of suits. Who knew if they were all in on Mel and Curt's plan? Two of them looked my way then averted their sights to three young brunettes who clicked past the ticket booth in their black spiked heels.

"Find him and bring him to me *now*, damn it!" Mr. Red Tie growled at the telephone, white-knuckling the receiver.

I left the building and headed around to the back. I wasn't sure if any of those guys would be following me, but I didn't want to stick around to find out. I hid beyond the amber ring of light cast by a nearby streetlamp and huffed, out of breath. I was alone, but I could still hear the chatter of the people who lingered around the front of the building. I pulled out my notebook and jotted down the names and descriptions of the men I'd encountered, including Mr. Red Tie. If they were all affiliated with Darin, then they might know something about Luanda too. *And who's this girlfriend? Is Darin playing around?* Whoever she was, she was in deep trouble with these cats. I had a sinking feeling about all this, and it made my skin crawl. I needed to get to Darin.

A flickering glow behind my feet caught my attention. Turning, I noticed a wide metal grate, where a frosted rectangular egress window sat below at the base of the building's brick wall. I knelt and peered at the window from the grating. I couldn't see anything, but I guessed the privacy probably meant it was a bathroom or one of the changing areas. The metal grating shined like new; the installation looked very recent. I recalled sometime last year, when Sam was grumbling something about special new building codes that had taken effect around the city. If these things were part of the new regulations, I could understand Sam's frustration. They sure looked like more trouble than they were worth. I tried pulling open the grate, but it was locked and wouldn't budge.

I stood and looked around the base of the building. Another similar metal grate was set into the concrete about fifty feet away. It, too, shined like a new addition. Peering through the grate, I spotted another frosted egress window. This one was open and offered a view of a long metal bench and a wall of steel lockers in the room beyond. *I wonder...*

Looking left and right, I listened for sounds then tugged on the grate. To my surprise, it flipped open with ease. Light from the window cast a dim light into the recessed area that looked just wide enough for one person to kneel. After another quick check over my shoulder, I slid into the recess and looked through the window. The small locker room was empty, save for two red boxing gloves tossed haphazardly onto the grimy tile floor. One end of the long wooden bench was pushed up against the door.

I was a little too late. But Curt and Mel didn't need to know that. I pulled back from the window and slid it shut. Two sets of dirty, sweaty handprints smeared the glass. Darin had escaped, all right, and he was on the run from these guys. *But why?*

I crawled out of the recess and closed the grate. My next stop would be Cheryl's place, but I had to rethink things. There was a chance I might find Darin there, too, and I still wasn't entirely sure about his motives. What was his connection to these guys, and how did it all connect to Cheryl or Lu? If he wasn't straight, things could turn south fast, and after remembering what Ali had done to Foreman at last year's Rumble in the Jungle event, there was no way I was going to get into a brawl with any chiseled boxing champion. I had to prepare for the worst, and it was times like these when reinforcements were necessary. *I guess I'll be visiting some friends tonight, after all.*

CHAPTER 5

My luck had run out—at least, when it came to cab drivers. According to the dispatch office, Sid was driving a passenger to Manhattan, and I didn't have time to wait around for him. So I hailed the first taxi I could get. The driver who pulled up, a woman who looked about my age, took one glance at me, scowled, then sped ahead to pick up a man several feet away from me. I sneered.

I knew that cabbie's look. My skin was obviously too dark for her backseat. *Whatever.* That ignorant turkey was living in the wrong city to think that she would never run into people who didn't look like her. I wasn't surprised. If anything, I was more annoyed, because it meant I would have to wait for another taxi. Meanwhile, Darin Rivers was out there somewhere, and it was almost midnight.

Fifteen minutes later, another taxi pulled up along the curb in front of me. I was alone this time, but a cynical part of me expected the cabbie to zoom off as well. The young, pudgy driver looked at me through his tortoise-shell glasses then lifted his hand with an expectant gesture.

Huh. So he really is waiting on me. I flung open the back door and climbed in. "Thanks."

"*¿Dónde tienes que ir?*" the cabbie asked, eyeing me in the rearview mirror, from which a pair of fuzzy dice and a beaded Dominican Republic flag symbol necklace hung.

"Kronos Lounge, and step on it," I said.

His brow furrowed. "*¿Qué?*"

I blinked several times then realized this guy probably didn't know a lick of English. Sighing, I tapped my finger against my temple as I concentrated, putting my rusty high school Spanish to work. "Kronos Lounge *en* Queens Village. Um… *cerca… de la…* uh… *esquina de…* Hempstead Avenue *y* Springfield Boulevard."

The cabbie looked deep in thought for a moment and scratched one of his thick sideburns that ran out from beneath his dark-blue flatcap.

"Kronos... Hempstead..." He suddenly perked up and snapped his fingers. "*Ah, lo tengo.*"

I nodded. "*Sí.* Uh... *y hazlo...* um... *rápido por favor.*"

"*¡Entendido!*" He gave me a thumbs-up and floored the gas pedal.

I leaned my head back and let out a deep sigh. I hadn't planned to be working my brain so hard tonight. I unwrapped a Tootsie Roll from my coat pocket and indulged in its chewy, chocolatey goodness. It was just what I needed to relax, gather myself, and mentally prepare for the possible trouble ahead. During the trip, I managed to learn the cabbie's name was Matteo Fuentes and he'd been living in New York for about six months. Although his English skills were beyond lacking, he seemed nice enough and patiently tolerated my slow, awkward Spanish. He didn't know the boroughs as well as Sid did, but he drove just as fast. And that was fine with me.

At 11:50 p.m., the cab stopped beside a car parked under the amber glow of a lone streetlamp in front of a long, grungy graffiti-covered strip building on Hempstead Avenue. Several other cars were parked along the curb on both sides of the wide street. A large burly man in a striped long-sleeved polo shirt stood outside one of the nondescript units, which sat between a shuttered beauty salon and a

vacant unit with a For Rent sign hanging in its
barred window. Faint neon-blue light glowed from
between the grates of the barred metal door behind
the man, who stood stock-still with his thick arms
crossed. His head moved steadily left and right as he
surveyed the area and scanned the occasional
passerby. His gaze eventually landed in my direction.

"Um... *espera... aquí... por favor*," I said to
Matteo. "Ah... *luego*... uh... *vamos a* Soundview."
No way was I going to risk trying to wait on another
cab just to save a couple quarters.

"*Sí.*" He put the car in park.

I got out and stepped onto the curb, my feet
crushing the cigarette butts and a soggy newspaper
that littered the curb. The pleasant aroma of eggrolls
and steamed vegetables coming from the Chinese
takeout joint across the street quickly overtook the
stench of the gutter funk.

I approached the man standing in front of the
barred door. Above him, a small painted sign read
Kronos Lounge. The sleeves of his polo shirt fit him
snugly, revealing enough muscle definition to make
any unruly drunk or hoodlum think twice about
acting a fool. *Thank goodness he's working tonight.*

The man's brow furrowed, then he did a double
take. "Tootsie? That you?"

I quirked a smile. "Mitts. Just the guy I need.
Been a while, eh?"

"Too damn long. Oh, and Roy's been a basket case since he hasn't heard from you."

I rolled my eyes. "Yeah, yeah. So what else is new? Look, I need you to do me a solid."

One of his eyebrows arched. "I must be hearing things. You never ask for nothin'."

"Yeah, well… it's not often I go after boxing champions either."

"Say what?"

"Look, I'm in a hurry. I need you, man. Now. Every second counts."

Mitts glanced left and right again then sighed. "I'm working the doors tonight, Tootsie. I can't just up and leave. You're gonna have to talk to my boss."

I scowled. "I ain't in the mood for *your boss's* jive talk. Go tell him you're sick or something. Just make it quick, will you? I'm still on the meter." I jabbed my thumb over my shoulder toward the waiting taxi.

Mitts hesitated. "Tootsie, I can't. I'm the only doorman he's got tonight."

I rubbed my hands over my face, exasperated. "I wouldn't be coming all the way here, asking you this, if it wasn't important. I'm on a case, and I need you tonight. Besides, you and I both know that Roy always has a backup plan."

His square jaw tightened. "All right, fine. I guess I got the sniffles, huh?" He turned to the door. "Be right back."

"And don't you *dare* tell Roy I'm here!" I yelled over the cacophony of people's voices and disco music that poured out as he opened the door.

The minutes ticked by as I anxiously paced back and forth, checking my watch. The noise of the lounge's interior blared again as the entrance door swung back open, and Mitts stepped out, followed by Roy Ellison, the owner, who looked too flustered at Mitts to notice me. Roy, who was of average height and build, was wearing one of his many brightly colored gaudy leisure suits. *Always so full of himself, that Roy, right down to his fashion sense.* Groaning, I lowered the brim of my hat over my eyes and rushed back to the taxi.

"What do you mean you're sick?" Roy exclaimed while Mitts continued toward the taxi, not looking back. "I need a bouncer! You can't just leave!"

"Man, I'm about to puke all over this sidewalk if I stand out here any longer," Mitts croaked, opening the passenger door. "Call Collins. He's probably home. Tell 'im you'll pay a bonus, and he'll get here in ten minutes flat."

"*B-Bonus!* You crazy, man?" Roy stared wide-eyed at him. Mitts squeezed in beside me and closed the door. I kept the brim of my hat lowered and turned my head away. *Please don't let Roy see me. Please don't let Roy see me.*

"Hey, hold on—who's the broad?" Roy asked.

Mitts gulped. "Uh… my nurse."

"She don't look like—"

"*¡Ve ahora!*" I yelled to Matteo.

Roy gasped. "Wait. Is that—"

"*¡Sí!*" Matteo yanked the shifter into drive and punched the gas, jolting Mitts and me backward against the backseat. I raised the brim of my hat and looked out the rear window at Roy standing in the street, throwing his hands up in defeat. I exhaled a deep sigh.

"What are you trying to do? Get me fired?" Mitts asked once we were well on our way.

I blew a raspberry. "Roy ain't gonna fire his best friend."

"Tch. The way he's been acting, I wouldn't be surprised. You should've just let me tell him you were here. He might've chilled out a bit."

"No. He would want a novel-sized explanation, and there's no time for that. Anyway, it's his own fault that he still can't get it through his thick skull that my line of work demands long hours, and I'm rarely home, which is why I keep missing his calls."

Mitts shrugged and shook his head. "Hey, he loves you. Can you blame him?"

I wrinkled my nose. "Ugh. He's nothing but a big baby." Love was a strange thing that I'd never taken the time to explore at great length. Especially when I had more fun and interesting things to stimulate my mind, like solving mysteries, bringing bad guys to justice, and helping people. It was hard to believe that Roy, that snot-nosed neighborhood bully, had ended up becoming a good-looking Casanova who was also a successful business owner. Why he kept wasting his time chasing after some boring private detective with no social life instead of all the good-looking bombshells he'd seemed to attract without even trying was beyond me.

"All right, so you mind telling me what in the hell you've roped me into?" Mitts asked.

We crossed the Whitestone Bridge into the borough of the Bronx, and I gave Matteo the address to Cheryl's place in Soundview. Then I filled Mitts in on my misadventures at Sunnyside Garden Arena.

"Darin Rivers..." He rubbed his chin, his eyes glazing over in thought. A corner of his mouth tugged upward, revealing a faint dimple in his left cheek. "So he's back, eh? Man, that cat's been outta the scene for a while."

I raised my eyebrows. "You know him?"

"He was the talk of the local gyms, up until a couple years ago. I watched him train a few times, back in his heyday, and man, was he something else. People used to call him Rocket Rivers because of his quick hands and feet. Top it all off, he was a southpaw. Everyone thought he'd go pro one day.

Maybe even get the opportunity to fight Ali or Frazier."

"What happened?"

Mitts shrugged. "He was damn good, but he had a temper. Beat up a cop pretty badly over a speeding ticket, and that got him put away for a while. His career was over before it began. People forgot about him and moved on to the next young sensation, and he pretty much disappeared from the boxing scene."

"I guess he's trying to make a comeback, eh? But it seems he might be running with the wrong company."

"It's a shame, y'know? All that talent." Mitts furrowed his brow. "Wait a minute. So is that why I'm here? You want me to take him out?"

"You're my reinforcement. I've never had a case like this before, and I think I'm in over my head with this one. I don't know Darin's motives, and if he has a short temper like you say, then things might get a little rough."

"Since when has a little rough stuff ever stopped you? Anyway..." He grimaced. "Don't you have a gun?"

"Yeah, I do, but I really don't want to have to use it on him, especially since he's a possible prime suspect. Furthermore..." I tapped the side of my head with my finger. "I kinda need this brain for this line of work, y'know? I don't need it bashed in by a pair of 'rocket fists.'"

Mitts snorted. "And what am I? Chopped liver? You think I don't care about messing up this pretty mug?"

The big bear was charming in his own way, but parts of his face bore old battle scars and bruises from his many years of street fighting and working as a bouncer. "Of course I care. But the fact is, you'd stand a better chance at knocking him out with those sledgehammer fists of yours than anyone else I know."

"I ain't a boxer. I mean, I did it for fun a few times, but that ain't me."

"You boxed. You brawled. You wrestled. No matter how you put it, you're a man of the streets who's made a lot of people see stars. Now, I need you to do it one more time."

He let out a deep sigh and rubbed his hand down his face. "You're killin' me, Tootsie. Y'know that?"

I smiled at him. "I'll make it worth your while. Promise."

CHAPTER 6

We pulled up in front of a six-story apartment building in Soundview around a quarter after midnight. As I reached for my wallet, Mitts forked over the cab fare to Matteo. "Gray-see-us," he said, opening the door.

Taking the cash, Matteo scrunched his brow at him then looked at me.

Rolling my eyes, I waved my hand apologetically. "Ah... *no le hagas caso, por favor,*" I said then slid out of the cab after Mitts.

Grinning, Matteo gave me a thumbs-up. "*Todo está bien. Adiós.*" He sped off down the street.

I glanced at Mitts flatly. "You didn't have to do that," I said then hustled along the short walkway toward the building's entrance.

"Do what? Pay the fare?" He huffed, remaining several footsteps behind me. "You're sticking your neck out tonight, Tootsie. It's the least I could do."

"Yeah, but I'm technically hiring you." I stopped in front of an old, weathered doorbell panel affixed to the wall. One corner of the panel had rusted off, while three other corner screws fought to hold the thing in place. I ran my finger along the penned names that sat behind grimy, bronze-trimmed plates.

"Hey, we're friends. I'm doing you a solid, remember? Besides, I'm trying to be all gentlemanly like."

I slid a dubious glance over my shoulder at him. "You trying to be a gentleman is like trying to teach a caveman how to wear a tuxedo."

Mitts laughed. "Hey, c'mon. I ain't that bad."

"Riiight." I located Cheryl's name—apartment 5B—and pressed the button beside it with my thumb. I waited a few moments, but there was no answer. Grumbling, I pushed it again. *I hope I'm not too late…*

I stared at the panel's speaker, waiting eagerly to hear a woman's voice, but all was silent.

Did she go out? I pushed the button again and again, but there was still no reply. I clenched my jaw. *Am I too late? Is Darin there? Has something happened to her?* I had to know for sure. I turned away from the doorbell listing and paced in front of the entrance doors.

"Either Cheryl's not home, or she's in big trouble. We have to get in there somehow," I said to Mitts.

He shrugged. "Who's this Cheryl chick? I thought we were going after Darin?"

"I've reason to believe that Darin might be up there with her—if she really is home. He might be holding her hostage, for all I know."

"Or, y'know, she could just not be home." He assessed the door then shook his head. "Reinforced steel. Ain't no way we're busting our way through there."

I thought for a moment. I was running out of options. Gritting my teeth, I kicked the door in frustration.

"Hey, look."

I swiveled my gaze to Mitts, who was focused on something in the street. I turned just in time to see a taxi cab park along the curb.

"Maybe it's Cheryl," Mitts said.

The taxi door flew open, and a pair of legs with one red high-heeled shoe attached fluttered kicks in midair.

Maybe... I elbowed Mitts in the arm then muttered, "Be cool. Act like we're looking for my keys." I fished my keyring from my trench coat pocket and began pawing through it.

"Okay..." Mitts watched me curiously. Then he shrugged and reached into one of the deep pockets of his trousers. He yanked out a wad of keys secured around a single ring that was attached to a chain.

I did a double take. "Geez Louise! You got the keys to every building in Queens or something?"

"Naw. See, this one's for Kronos's office. And this one's to the storage room. And this one here's to my apartment. And this one's—"

"Never mind." I glanced back at the parked taxi, where a skinny man in a funky blue suit hopped out from the rear driver's-side door and raced around to the other door with the mysterious pair of legs.

"C'mon, baby. Stop being like that," Skinny said. "Where's your other shoe?"

The legs gave an energetic kick that sent the remaining shoe flying, and a young woman in a sparkly red Halston dress leaned out of the cab. The man scooped her out onto the sidewalk, and she fell against him, giggling.

"Less go up'n 'ave a drink, Big Daddy," Ms. Red slurred at her escort.

He wrapped a long black coat around her shoulders, grabbed a tiny clutch purse from the back of the cab, and stuck it in one of the coat's pockets. "I think you've had enough for one night," he replied, steadying her on her feet. He headed toward the entrance, his gaze darting left and right, as he was clearly looking for a way to escape. He stopped before me and Mitts. "Hey, you guys live here?"

"Yeah, why?" I asked.

"Uh, you mind getting Vivian here up to her apartment? I, um… got a family emergency I need to take care of."

I deflated a little, realizing that this woman wasn't Cheryl. "Sure. You got her key? It'll take us all night to find ours." I prodded my thumb at Mitts, and he cracked a gap-toothed smile, holding up his jangling wad of keys.

Skinny reached into Vivian's coat pocket and pulled out the clutch purse, which was made of the same sparkly fabric as her minidress. Without looking inside, he simply handed it to me. "Here."

"Uh, thanks." I took the purse, quirking an eyebrow at him. By the way the man kept his gaze averted, I wondered whether he really had an emergency or was simply in a hurry to escape this woman. My cynical side was betting on the latter.

Skinny shot Vivian a spooked look then did an about-face and bolted back to the taxi faster than a greyhound. As the cab pulled away, Vivian's other shoe sailed out of open back window and bounced along the sidewalk.

"Heeey! Whereya goin'? Come back!" Vivian stretched her hand toward the taxi as it screeched around a corner and was gone. She tottered forward, and Mitts caught her midfall.

I opened the clutch purse and looked inside to find a lipstick, a compact, a loose dime, and a thin gold-colored wallet with "V.N." stamped in one corner in fancy monogramed lettering. Beneath the wallet was a tarnished bronze unmarked key. *But to which apartment?* I scanned the doorbell listing and located the only name with "V.N.": V. North, apartment 2D.

"You get Vivian. I'll get her purse and shoes," I said to Mitts as I stuck the key into the keyhole and twisted it. The lock clicked open. When he didn't answer, I looked over my shoulder at him.

Vivian stared heavy-eyed at Mitts and chortled. "You're cute."

Mitts grinned sheepishly as he continued holding her in his arms, his eyes clearly drawn to the cleavage revealed by her dress's plunging neckline.

"Mitts! Eyes up." I snapped my fingers.

He blinked and looked my way. "She said I was cute."

"Yeah, and she's also drunk as a skunk."

The apartment elevator stank like piss and mildew, and the pulleys screamed all the way to the third floor. It beat hauling a drunk up the stairs, though. Vivian invited Mitts for a drink and even stoked his manly ego when she called him Big Daddy, but Mitts managed to peel her off him and stuff her through her doorway without getting caught up in her spell. I was proud of the big bear. I tossed the purse and shoes after her and slammed the door.

"Now, to Cheryl," I grumbled. The elevator had moved down to the second floor, so I headed for the stairwell.

"Ugh, do we have to take the stairs?" Mitts whined as he followed me reluctantly.

"Well, I sure ain't gonna wait around for that foul elevator again." I opened the door to the dimly lit stairwell, my nose immediately sensing that it had been frequently used as a lavatory. I climbed the stairs two at a time, dodging stray garbage and broken toys until I reached the fifth floor. I looked down the pit of stairs to find Mitts still on the third floor, steadily trudging his way up.

"C'mon, man! You're supposed to be in shape!" I called.

He huffed. "I didn't train to run a damned marathon!"

"Geez Louise. It's just stairs." I opened the exit door and stepped out into a narrow hallway clad in grungy polished brick and lit by the only two of the six dome lights still burning in the cracked yellow ceiling. The stench of the stairwell was quickly overpowered by the delectable aroma of meats and cooked peppers wafting into the hallway from one of the apartments. Mitts finally joined me and bent over, panting, letting the stairwell's exit door crash closed behind him. I turned to shush him, placing my finger over my lips, then slinked down the hallway. I halted in front of 6B.

Mitts came lumbering up behind me.

I pounded on the door. "Cheryl! You there? What's going on?"

"Leave!" a man's gruff voice boomed from inside the apartment.

"Darin?" I called.

"I said leave!"

I pushed back from the door. It had to be him. *Am I too late?* "I'm here to see Cheryl. If she's in trouble, I'm going to call the police!"

The lock turned immediately, and the door opened a crack. Half of a man's head appeared, part of his face shadowed. A dark-brown eye glared at me. "Cheryl ain't here. Get lost," he growled.

My throat tightened again, and I wedged my foot in the door. "Darin? Is that you?"

The man scowled. Something small and silver glinted in the light as he slipped his right hand behind his back. "This is your last warning."

This guy was packing, and he meant business. I glanced at Mitts and jerked my head toward the door. Mitts lifted one massive leg and drove it into the scarred wood like a pile driver. The door flew open, splintering at its hinges as it hit the wall, then bounced back. Before it could slam shut again, the side of Mitts's solid forearm stopped it. He charged into the apartment, with me right on his heels, my hand already on the butt of my .38 inside my trench coat.

Cigarette smoke hung in the air. A man, too bulky to be Darin, stumbled backward as we erupted into the room. He held one arm back, shoving a woman—Cheryl, I assumed—behind him, as if protecting her. I recognized the man from the fight. Towel Guy, one of Darin's cornermen. *Did Darin send him here to do his dirty work? None of this makes sense.*

Towel Guy shoved Cheryl away, whipped out a revolver from behind him, and aimed it at Mitts and me. "Take another step, and you'll both be eating lead," he warned.

"Put the gun away," I said, keeping my hand poised in my trench coat. "Where's Darin? Why are you doing this?"

"I ain't tellin' ya shit. Now get outta here!" His dark eyes focused on me.

"Don't shoot! Don't shoot!" Cheryl yelped and scrambled back behind the couch.

With an angry roar, Mitts charged Towel Guy. I ducked out of the line of fire and yanked out my gun. A shot rang out—a shot that wasn't mine—and popcorn-ceiling dust showered down like snow flurries. Steady ringing resonated from my ears as the acrid stench of gunsmoke overtook the room's stink of cigarettes. The two men clashed like bulls. Mitts held Towel Guy's gun arm down and away, while Towel Guy struggled to lift his arm.

I rushed toward the men and delivered a spinning kick to Towel Guy's wrist, sending his little .32 flying. Now, evenly matched, the two men went sprawling, trading blows. Towel Guy drove his fist into the side of Mitts's ribs. Huffing, Mitts doubled over for a second then lifted his head, giving the man a smile. It was one of those sadistic kind of smiles Mitts only did whenever he was shot up with adrenaline-fueled pleasure. Mitts lunged to his feet and clocked the other man solidly in his jaw. Spittle flying out of his mouth, Towel Guy spun like a top and dropped like a rock, out cold.

Not taking his eyes off the unconscious man, Mitts ran his thumb across his own bottom lip, swiping up blood. He looked at his thumb for a moment then blew a raspberry. "Aww, c'mon. That it? I was just having fun. You dragged me out here for this, Tootsie?"

I turned to Cheryl, who was curled up in a ball against the back of the couch. "Hey, you okay?"

Cheryl looked up with big, soft eyes. She had light-brown skin and a tiny mole on her jawline. She was the kind of pretty that tended to look good even without makeup. Still shaken, she didn't seem hurt.

"Look, whatever you want, take it. Just leave me alone. Please!" Cheryl held up her hands in surrender.

"Hey, chill out. We're not here to hurt you," I said.

She looked at Mitts and me warily then pushed herself up. As she moved around to the front of the couch, I followed. She sank down onto the cushions and groped her shaky hand around the side table until she found a pack of cigarettes. She tried to steady her hand as she fought to stick one of the bogeys in her mouth.

I retrieved the lighter from the side table, whipped up a flame with a flick of my thumb, and touched the tip of her cig.

"Thanks." She leaned back against the pillows, taking a drag, then exhaled a steady stream of smoke.

"I hope we don't get any visits from the neighbors." I grimaced.

Cheryl blew a raspberry. "The neighbors don't care. Shit far worse than this happens all the time somewhere in this building. People know not to nose around or snitch."

"Right…"

"So, you're not here to kill me. Who are you?"

"Of course we're not here to kill you. My name is Tootsie Carter. I'm a private detective. The big bear over there is my friend Mitts."

Mitts reached down and held the unconscious man up by two fistfuls of his shirt collar. "No wonder he fell so easily. This ain't Darin."

Cheryl turned her doe eyes on Mitts for a moment then looked back at me. "What do you want with Darin?"

"I'm actually looking for Luanda," I said.

Cheryl froze, the cigarette dangling from between her fingers. "Lu…"

"Her husband's worried sick about her. I've reason to believe she's with Darin or at least that he knows where she is."

Shaking her head, Cheryl took another drag. "I-I don't think she's with Darin."

I whipped out my notepad. "Why?"

"'Cause I just know, all right? She's my friend." Cheryl glared.

Mitts went to the door and fiddled with it, trying to shut it despite its damaged hinges.

"So, where do you think she is?" I asked Cheryl.

"I don't know… Look. What do you want from me? I haven't done anything wrong. Unlike my neighbors, I got nothing illegal going on."

"I need your cooperation. Luanda might be in trouble, and I'm trying to find her."

Cheryl looked at me long and hard then sighed. Her gaze averted to the floor. "He's going to kill her if I say anything," she said, just above a whisper.

I raised my eyebrows. "Who's going to kill her?"

Cheryl shrugged and shook her head. "Some guy Lu and I met at the gym Monday night. He seemed straight. Lu talked to him for a bit while I flirted with Darin. Next thing I know, she tells me she has to pick up something from the cleaners, leaves the gym, and that's the last I see of her."

I scribbled some notes. "Do you know which cleaners she went to?"

She spat out a stream of smoke. "If I knew that, I wouldn't be sitting here, worrying about my friend, now would I?"

"Fair enough. You remember what this guy looked like?"

"Yeah. Italian cat about yea tall. Average build. Dressed like a high roller."

"His name wouldn't happen to be Curt, would it?"

She shrugged. "No idea. He never said his name."

I wonder... My throat tightened as I jotted down notes, fearing the worst for Lu. *What kind of mess has she gotten mixed up in?* I thought.

The glowing tip of Cheryl's cigarette pulsated steadily. Her face went pale. "Look, I've said enough. Don't snitch to the cops. Please. I don't want my friend hurt."

"Don't worry. This is my case. The cops won't know anything until after I've solved it."

"Good. Because it's bad enough Alex is here. I'm worried about Lu."

"Alex?"

"Darin's trainer. That guy your boyfriend just clobbered." She jabbed her cig at Towel Guy snoozing on the floor.

I blinked several times. "T-Trainer?"

"Trainer?" Mitts echoed, looking at the both of us wide-eyed. "Geez, Darin must really be desperate for a comeback to hire this cat as a trainer."

"Alex is a swell guy," Cheryl said. "He and Darin are also close friends. Apparently, Darin told him to keep an eye on me tonight."

I guess Darin already knew something was about to go down. I approached Alex. I slapped his cheeks a few times, and he stirred briefly, but his eyes still didn't open. I definitely wasn't going to get anything out of him anytime soon. Sighing, I returned to Cheryl.

"Ehh... I won't tell Darin I knocked out his trainer if you don't." Mitts rubbed the back of his head, grimacing.

"Is he gonna be all right?" Cheryl asked me.

"He'll be fine. I was hoping to ask him some questions about Darin."

Cheryl stabbed the butt of her finished cigarette into a glass ashtray sitting on the side table. "He doesn't know where Darin is. Trust me. I already asked. He doesn't know about Lu either."

"Great..." I rubbed my chin. "Say, you know anything about Darin's girlfriend?"

Her eyes widened a moment, then her face went rigid. "No? Is he seeing someone? Did you see her?"

"No, but she's apparently in big trouble..."

"He told me he wasn't seeing anyone. He told me he loved me, and..." Scowling, she balled her fists. "If that bastard lied to me, I swear, I'll—"

"So, *you're* his girlfriend?"

"I thought I was. But if he's playing around, I ain't gonna stand for it."

"Where's this gym that you and Lu met Darin at?"

"Primo's Boxing Club, down in Hunt's Point."

"Oh, I know that place," Mitts said. "A lot of the heavy hitters hang out there."

I wrote the info in my notebook. "In any event, I don't think it's safe for you guys to stay here. There are some bad people who probably know where you live, and it's nothing for them to send some of their friends here to hurt you, or worse."

"Where the hell am I supposed to go?" She paused then perked up. "Maybe Alex can take me to Philly. That's where he and Darin are from."

"No. I don't want you guys to leave town. I might need you around in case I have more questions." I rubbed my chin. "I have a friend who owns a bar in Queens—Kronos Lounge. Ever heard of it?"

She looked thoughtful. "Sounds familiar. Haven't been out to Queens in a while."

"I'll give you the address. You guys go there and ask for Roy Ellison, the owner. Tell him Tootsie sent you and that you need a place to stay for a while. He'll set you up."

"Oh boy." Mitts rubbed the back of his head. "Roy ain't gonna like this, Tootsie."

"He won't, but it's necessary in order for me to solve this case. I'll talk to him about it later."

She cocked her head to the side. "Roy Ellison? You sure he'll believe me?"

"He better. And if he doesn't, he'll have to answer to me." I shook my fist. "And you can tell him I said that too."

"All right. I'll go. What about you?"

"I need to find Lu."

"I wish I knew where she was…" Cheryl sighed.

"You and me both. I'll find her. And I'll find Darin too." I wrote down the lounge address and handed it to Cheryl. "Pack light and leave as soon as you can."

She took the paper, stared at it a moment, then gave a slow nod. "I still don't know what the hell's going on, but okay." She got up from the couch and headed to her bedroom.

"So, any idea where we might find Darin?" Mitts asked.

"Looks like we might need to try Hunt's Point next." I sighed.

His face lit up as though he'd just won the lottery. "Sweet. My old playground."

"Your old playground? It's one of the most dangerous places in the city!"

"Exactly."

I rolled my eyes. "Right. Well, I'm sure you'll find yourself a nice mugger to rough up."

"Heh. There're far worse things than muggers out there." His grin broadened. "Sure beats standing outside a door all night, bored as hell."

"You mean, this wasn't enough action for you already?" I teased.

He snorted. "I'm just barely warmed up."

Cheryl came out of her room, her brown leather overnight bag slung over her shoulder. She looked at me expectantly.

"All packed? Good. Time to get outta here, now. We'll talk again later." I nudged Mitts. "Grab Alex, will you?"

"I'll go get us a cab," Cheryl said, heading to the apartment's exit. She stopped in front of the battered door, shook her head, and sighed.

"Um... sorry about your door," I said.

"Meh, I've had worse." She tossed me the key. "Try to lock it on your way out, will you?"

After Cheryl left, Mitts hefted Alex over his shoulder in a fireman's carry. Mitts grunted as he straightened, and he lumbered out the doorway. I followed and locked the door behind me. Thankfully, that was still functional.

Cheryl was waiting in the cab by the time Mitts and I got outside. Mitts dropped Alex in the backseat with Cheryl. I returned her key and shut the door. The cab zoomed off. After they were gone,

I turned to Mitts. "Time for us to take a joyride downtown."

Grinning, Mitts cracked his knuckles. "I'm ready."

I located the nearest pay phone and gave Sid a call.

CHAPTER 7

It was almost one in the morning when we arrived at Hunt's Point. Sid brought the cab to a stop along the curb in front of a run-down three-story residential brick building with boarded-up windows.

"Hey, I really appreciate you helping me out like this," I said.

"Y'know I wouldn't pass up the opportunity to drive you around, li'l lady." Sid laughed then shut off the meter.

Sid was technically supposed to be off the clock, but when he'd learned my call had come in through the dispatch office, he'd practically begged his boss to work extra. Thankfully, his boss was swell, because Sid had zoomed my way not long after I'd hung up the phone.

Mitts paid the fare and gave me a funny look. "You getting sweet on the old man, Tootsie?"

I wrinkled my nose. "Where'd you get that idea from?"

"Well, you know…"

"Ey!" Sid barked, glaring at Mitts from the rearview mirror. "Ms. Carter is a respectable young lady. You better treat her like one, or else." The way he said that, it sounded like he would probably follow through with his threat. And knowing a guy like Sid, he probably would too.

Pale faced, Mitts looked at him then gulped. "Y-Yes, sir."

My jaw dropped. *Wow.* If Sid could tame a wild beast like Mitts, then he was certainly the real deal.

Sid's forehead wrinkled. "By the way, Ms. Carter. If y'don't mind me askin', why'd you wanna come here at this hour? I mean, this place ain't called Street Walker's Paradise for nothin'."

I smiled reassuringly. "I'm on a case."

"A… case?"

"I'm a private detective."

His eyes went wider than saucers. "A detective… like… like Dick Tracy?"

I started. It was the last thing I'd expected to hear, especially from Sid. "Why... yes. Yes, actually."

Groaning, Mitts opened the door. "Please don't get her started on Dick Tracy."

"You got a problem with Dick Tracy, chump?" Sid glared at him again.

"N-No, sir," he muttered then slid out of the cab.

I smiled back at Sid. "You've got good taste. We'll have to talk later."

"Right on, doll. Y'know, I was five years old when the first strip came out in the papers, and I've been a fan ever since."

My jaw dropped. *The first strip? Wow, he must be a walking encyclopedia of all things Dick Tracy.* I inhaled a deep breath to calm my excited nerves and focused on the task at hand. Just having the opportunity to pick his brain made me all the more anxious to solve this case as fast as I could. I slid out of the cab.

"Hey, Sid, you wouldn't happen to know of any garment cleaners' places around this area, would you?" I asked, before closing the door.

He rubbed his chin a moment then perked up. "Let's see. There's Chester's Cleaners over on Bryant Avenue, Five-Star Cleaners just two blocks over on the corner of Randall and Faile, and then there's Clean as a Whistle on East 156th and Truxton."

I slid him a five-dollar tip through the bulletproof partition. "Thanks again. You've been a big help."

He took the money with a big grin. "Anytime, doll. By the way, if that chump over there ever gives you a hard time, you just let me know, eh?" He made a small head gesture to Mitts. "I'll show 'im why I was called Smashin' Sid back in my ol' boxing days."

I chuckled. "I'll keep that in mind. Catch you later."

After Sid sped off, Mitts exhaled a deep sigh.

"You all right?" I asked. "I've never seen you that spooked before."

"Yeah. That guy is a bulldog. I saw the look in his eyes. Let's just say that anyone from the street knows not to mess with guys like him."

"He's almost fifty."

"The older they are, the tougher they get."

I decided to leave it at that, but I couldn't help but imagine Sid clocking Mitts the same way Mitts had Alex. *My, that would be some sight.*

Mitts sneered. "What are you smiling about?"

I cleared my throat. "Nothing. Come on, there's work to do."

Primo's Boxing Club was tucked into an old, shabby building, one of the few structurally sound buildings remaining on the street. A graffiti-covered steel door covered the gym's entrance. A flimsy plastic sign hung from a wrought-iron holder that was attached above the security door. I turned and assessed the rest of the area. A lone streetlamp above a doorless abandoned car across the street threw a meager amber glow, but its light barely illuminated the street signs and building numbers. Occasional shadowy passersby skulked and sauntered along the sidewalk. Sirens echoed in the distance.

I whipped out my notebook from my trench coat pocket and reviewed my case notes. "So, let's see. Cheryl said Lu left the gym to pick up something from the cleaners. Sid said the closest one is Five-Star Cleaners, which is two blocks from here on Randall and Faile. I'm guessing she probably went to that one. If we trace her steps, we might find a clue."

"Sounds like a plan." Mitts nodded.

We headed up the dark, narrow street. Mitts, in his full-on bodyguard mode, walked a few paces behind me. I glanced over my shoulder. His eyes scanned the area. There was plenty for him to look at.

A group of women dressed in barely there miniskirts and halter tops stood along the curb, smoking cigarettes, chatting, and idling about like they were waiting for a cab. Most of the women ignored me and Mitts, save for one who looked old enough to be my great-great-grandma. She eyed Mitts and blew kisses at him, but thankfully, he ignored the cringe-worthy attention.

A frazzled, middle-aged man in a dirty, hole-ridden sweatshirt and ripped jeans huddled near the brick wall of a building, his knees drawn to his chest. He rocked back and forth nervously, muttering something incoherent. He looked in my direction. His pale, wrinkled face was caved in and almost skeletal. The whites of his eyes became more prominent as he cast me a blank stare. I grimaced. I'd busted enough junkies to know that look all too well.

The man's attention flicked to Mitts, and he stopped rocking, holding himself tighter. The man stopped mumbling, and his bottom lip quivered. Either that guy knew Mitts, or Mitts was just that intimidating. I pressed on with longer strides and faster steps. I was starting to wonder if Luanda had ever reached the cleaners at all.

The continuous wailing of emergency sirens echoed from several blocks away. The dark sky pulsated a faint eerie orange glow. Another building was burning somewhere. Not a day went by without news of arson or some other fire-related emergency happening around the city.

We reached Randall Avenue. Rusty stripped cars sat abandoned along the curb of the wide street.

Remnants of buildings lay in heaps of rubble in long-forgotten lots. This place looked like a war zone. *Could Luanda really have gone this way?*

"Heeey, foxy mama, where ya off ta so early dis fine mornin'?" a man's voice slurred.

We were a block away from Faile Street. An older man in a tattered trench coat sat against the base of a streetlight in front of a condemned three-story building. He chugged from something concealed in a brown paper bag. Mitts's presence loomed behind me, and I could sense his tension.

I gave the mysterious man a cautious stare then continued on my way without saying a word.

"Mighty pretty lady, ya are. Yessir," the man said, following me with his gaze. He grinned crookedly, revealing several missing teeth.

I focused my eyes ahead but kept the stranger in my peripheral vision.

"Ey, back off, old man. She's my girlfriend, you dig?" Mitts said.

I resisted the urge to spew out a most un-ladylike response.

The man whistled. "Daaamn, I picked th' right spot, then. Lotta fiiiine honeybees come walkin' dis way. Maybe one o' them'll be my girlfriend, too, huh?" He laughed.

Mitts snorted. "Out here in these parts? Depends on how much bread you got."

He took a long swig. "Y'know, I saw dis one broad earlier. Real sweet thing. Looked like a... angel. Sooo perfect. Was gonna ask her t' marry me, but she had ta go an' run off..."

Good for her. I caught shadowy movements in an abandoned lot next to the building. Moments later, the movement stopped, blending with the rest of the darkness.

"Them's the breaks." Mitts chuckled.

"Hah! I think I seen her in a movie. I don't see no pretty broads like dat 'cept in movies."

"Did you get her autograph?" Mitts joked.

"Naw..."

Wait a minute... I halted and looked back at the stranger, who enjoyed another chug of his mysterious drink. I was about to question him about the pretty woman he'd seen when the shadowy figures appeared again and emerged from the lot. Three young men who looked barely in their twenties stepped into the dim light. They were clad in denim vests and bearing colors—red bandannas. Two of them displayed the bandannas prominently around their foreheads, and the oldest-looking one had it tied around his forearm. They crowded the stranger.

"Hey, old man!" One of the youths kicked him in the ribs. "We told you once to get your crazy ass off our turf."

The stranger groaned and curled into a ball. "C'mon, I ain't do nothin'!" he whined.

"Guess we gotta teach you a lesson," another kid said, then he punched him in the stomach a few times.

Clenching my jaw, I exchanged glances with Mitts. The old man just might know something about Luanda. It was worth finding out. Mitts seemed to have read my mind, because he was already waggling his eyebrows at me, cracking his knuckles.

I sighed and gave him a nod, with a slight flick of my wrist. *Yeah, yeah. Go have your little fun.*

Grinning, Mitts approached the group. He tapped the back of one of the youths. "Hey, quit botherin' the old man."

The kid spun around. He was the youngest looking of the bunch and wore his red bandanna around his forehead. He looked Mitts up and down, and his jaw dropped open. "Oh, shi—"

Mitts did a double take. "Theo? That you?"

The kid shook his head. He stepped back, pulled out a pair of brass knuckles from his pocket, and hastily slid them on. "I don't know what you're talkin' about, man. Get outta here."

Theo's friends abandoned the stranger and confronted Mitts. They, too, gave him the once-over but didn't appear intimidated.

"You wanna be next, chump?" the older kid warned, flicking out a large switchblade from his back pocket. His other friend did the same and sidled behind Mitts, holding the blade to his back.

I lifted an eyebrow.

Mitts held up his hands slowly, eyeing the three. "Hey, now. We can do this the easy way, or—"

"Shut up," the older kid barked. He glanced in my direction then smirked. "Damn. What do we have here?"

Why Mitts didn't waste these three punks already, I didn't know, but it was really starting to annoy me. It was just my luck that Mitts happened to know one of the thugs. With my head lifted, I stood before the oldest gang member. He held the knife in a way that showed he had some skill with it, but he was an amateur compared to some of the junkies and ex-military criminals I'd seen during my short time on the force. I kept my main focus on him and the weapon in my peripheral vision. "Look, I don't want any trouble tonight. So I suggest you three just crawl on back to your dark hidey-hole where you came from and leave us and the old man alone."

The older kid grinned then laughed mockingly. "Feisty broad. I like that. How 'bout it, baby? Let's tangle."

I narrowed my eyes. "I'd rather kiss a dead rat."

His smile turned smug, and he stepped a little closer, his knife now pointed at me. His two friends flanked Mitts.

I cast a glance at Mitts. His head turned slightly, his gaze swiveling between the three young men again. Then he met my eyes for a second, and I practically heard his silent message: *"My turn."*

In one motion, Mitts spun, grabbing his rear attacker's knife hand, and torqued it until the weapon dropped. The kid yelped, and Mitts hurled him into Theo like a football. The two young men crashed onto the sidewalk.

The oldest one growled, grabbed my arm, then tugged me closer. He brought the edge of the knife to my throat. "Hey, cool it, chump, or your girlfriend's gonna need stitches!"

Mitts halted and watched him carefully.

Eyeing the knife, I inhaled. Then I grabbed his wrist with my free hand, holding him firmly, while I yanked my other hand out of his tight grip. I spun, keeping the knife in sight, and gave his wrist a sharp twist.

Crack.

The knife dropped, and the kid howled. He keeled over and held his disabled hand. He looked back at me with fire in his eyes. "Bitch!" He gritted his teeth then straightened again.

I stabbed my leg into his gut with a bone-crushing side kick, my tough boot folding him back over like a book and knocking the wind out of him. His eyes bugged out, and he staggered backward. I whipped out my gun and aimed it at him. "Still wanna tangle?"

His face turned snow white, and his one good hand shot up in surrender. "H-Hey, baby... easy... easy with that!" he said between gasps.

I scowled. "Don't call me baby. Now get outta here, sucker, before I pump you full of lead. And don't let me catch you or your friends' ugly mugs around here again, dig?"

He swallowed once then took a nervous step back.

"Scram!" I clicked off the safety.

The kid turned tail and ran, tripping over his two friends. He stumbled but quickly recovered and bolted down the sidewalk. His friends struggled to their feet and hurried after him. Soon, the three disappeared around the corner.

Sighing, I reset the safety and put away my gun.

Mitts raised his eyebrows. "Whoa. Who are you? Bruce Lee? Those were some bad moves. Where'd you learn that?"

I gave him a coy grin. "I was one of the few students who actually paid attention in self-defense class at the academy."

"That's dynamite."

"Anyway, I'm more partial to Jim Kelly."

"Oh yeah. He's a bad mother too."

"And he's *fine*."

Mitts laughed. "Don't tell Roy that."

"Roy can stick it up his nose."

"That's not very ladylike."

I snorted. "I'm not a lady today."

He gave me a funny look. "Okay…"

Mitts stood guard as I approached the old man, who was leaning on his elbow, holding his ribs. He looked up at me in awe. "Man… you two are somethin' all right…" He winced suddenly.

"You gonna be okay?" I asked, cocking my head to the side.

"Maybe… I'm just… tired…"

I chewed my bottom lip. "Hey, don't sleep on me now. I need some answers."

He closed his eyes and smiled. "Anything… for you… sweet thing…"

"The pretty lady you saw earlier. Do you remember where she went?"

"Mmm…" he mumbled. "Somewhere dat way…" He flicked his wrist in the direction farther down the street. "Think she said somethin' 'bout… gettin' some clothes. Don't think she got very far, though…"

I arched an eyebrow. "Why not?"

"Got picked up by some nice-lookin' cat... Had a funky walk."

"Was he driving a car?"

"Dunno. Maybe... I'm so... tired." The man's face turned paler.

A sinking feeling started in my gut. I checked the man for injuries. He had multiple bruises around his ribs and midsection, and a few ribs were broken as well. The severity of those injuries must've been internal. While Mitts stayed behind to keep an eye on him, I rushed to the nearest telephone booth and called an ambulance. When I returned to the old man, he was already dead.

CHAPTER 8

Lu's trail ended up going cold in Hunt's Point, and after I'd called in the old man's death to the chief, Mitts and I took a bus back to Queens. Before I decided to call it a night and head home, I needed to take care of one last thing. Around a quarter to three in the morning, we stepped off the bus at the corner near Kronos Lounge. As we walked, Mitts stuffed his hands in his pockets and looked ahead, his face clouded with gloom.

"What's up?" I asked.

"I'm fine," he muttered.

"Don't sound like it. You still bent up about the old man?"

"Naw... well, yeah... well... I mean...   I'm just..." He sighed. "Damn... I can't believe Theo joined a gang."

I scrunched my brow. "You mean that kid you knew? What was up with him, anyway?"

"I've known Theo since we were kids. My grandma used to babysit us after school sometimes. Theo was swell. I was eight years older than him, but we still had fun playing together. He always looked up to me like a big brother. I never had a sibling, so he pretty much took that role."

"When did you last see him?"

"After I left home."

"You mean ran away."

He bristled. "Hey, I was sixteen and stupid. But there ain't no harder lesson than life, I'll tell ya what."

"You'd think after thirteen years, he'd be happy to see you."

Mitts frowned. "Yeah... I don't get it."

"Maybe he felt lonely after you left. No more, uh... 'positive'—in a manner of speaking—role models to look up to, so he eventually turned to alternatives."

He averted his gaze to the ground and sighed. "I wish there was something I could do to help him. He don't deserve that life."

I shook my head. "He's gotta help himself first. Maybe now that he's seen you again, he'll rethink his choices."

Mitts looked back at me pleadingly. "Can you at least make sure he doesn't get charged for murder? I mean, he was the only one in the group who didn't actually touch the guy."

"I can't make any promises. But I didn't mention him when I talked to the chief. Let's just hope that if his friends end up getting caught, they don't rat Theo out."

"Yeah..." Mitts said in a choked-up voice.

We arrived at Kronos Lounge. Only a few cars remained parked along the curb, and no new patrons were on the way inside. Collins, another of Roy's doormen, leaned against the wall next to the entrance, looking more bored than a kid in an empty room. He saw us and perked up, pushing off the wall.

"Mitts? What are you doing here? Roy said you were sick," Collins said.

"I was. Now I'm not." He flashed a gap-toothed grin.

Collins's gaze bounced from Mitts to me, then his eyes widened. "Wait... Were you two—"

"Hey, lay off that jive talk," I warned. "Is Roy still here?"

Collins nodded. "Yeah, but he's not in a good mood."

"When is he ever?" Mitts muttered, rolling his eyes.

"Eh, a couple came here earlier, looking for him." Collins swiveled his gaze to me. "They said you sent them here."

"I did." I nodded. "I need to see them."

He held his hands up in surrender. "You're gonna have to talk to Roy about that. Like I said, he ain't in a good mood."

"I'm sure I'll be able to lighten his mood."

"Yeah, I hope so. Roy promised me some extra bread for taking over tonight." He cast an annoyed look at Mitts then opened the door for me.

I entered, while Mitts stayed outside and chatted with Collins. The loud, upbeat dance music from earlier had been replaced by a low, mellow, relaxing buzz that matched the lounge's dim lighting. A scantily clad bar girl was leaned across the counter, chatting with an inebriated patron slumped over his drink, barely keeping himself steady on his high-backed stool. A few late-night stragglers occupied tables, making the most of their last-call liquor. A woman wearing a bright-yellow jumpsuit swayed awkwardly back and forth to the jukebox's slow tunes on the empty dance floor.

I didn't see Cheryl or Alex, so I strode toward the back, passed the restrooms, and reached a closed door labelled Private. I tried the door, but it was locked, so I pounded on it with my fist. "Roy! Open up!"

Moments later, the door unlocked and swung open. "Hey, I said I was bus—" Roy appeared, dressed to the nines in his bright-green leisure suit, his half-unbuttoned shirt revealing a flashy gold chain strung around his neck. His handsome brown eyes burned with rage as he chewed on a toothpick, which bobbed up and down from his mouth. He took one look at me, and the anger ebbed like a calming storm. His eyes widened as if he were shocked to see me alive, and he plucked the toothpick from his mouth. "T-Tootsie? Holy—"

Sighing, I crossed my arms. "Nice to see you too." I craned my neck, trying to look past him. "Where are they?"

"Who?"

"Cheryl and Alex, that's who."

He rubbed his hands over his face. "Oh, for crying out loud... Do you have any idea how much trouble you've put me through?"

"What trouble? All you had to do was to put 'em up somewhere safe till I came."

"First, you take my best bouncer during one of my busiest nights, then you send some random people down here for me to hide away because of another one of your jive 'cases.'"

I scowled. "It's an important case! A woman's gone missing, and I need those two for information. You better not have let them go."

He leaned against the doorframe and looked me up and down. "They're here."

"Good." I pushed past him. "I need to talk—"

"Hey." He placed his hands on my shoulders, stopping me. "Can you just… wait a minute?"

I glared. "Did you not hear me the first time? I'm on an important case. A woman's gone missing, and some dangerous people are looking for Cheryl. I don't have time to wait a minute."

"Damn it, Tootsie! Stop!" He tightened his grip.

"Let go of me."

His nostrils flared. "Will you at least listen to me?"

"Depends on what you have to say."

His gaze dulled, and his hands fell away from my shoulders. He didn't move from the doorway, though. "Look, I don't know what in the hell is going on, but you need to slow down."

I groaned. "What are you talking about?"

"I'm talking about you. When was the last time you got some sleep?"

"I took a nap early yesterday."

"Yeah? Well, I called you yesterday, and you didn't pick up. Are you ignoring me?"

"No, I was obviously either asleep or busy. You know this."

His jaw clenched. "Maybe I *don't* know. You don't tell me anything."

"Who are you? My mother?"

"C'mon, Tootsie. When are you gonna give me a chance?"

I grimaced. This helpless romantic was headstrong and not backing down. "There ain't no chance. Look, I don't have time to talk about this right now. I really need to see Cheryl and Alex."

He looked at me skeptically. "Can we talk afterwards?"

"I'll think about it."

He grumbled under his breath. "They're down there." He prodded his thumb toward a closed door at the back of the office.

I smirked, pinching his cheek. "So you *are* good for something."

He wrinkled his nose and pulled his face away. "Ugh. I hate it when you do that."

My smirk turned coyer. "I know."

He grunted then unlocked the door. "I'll be waiting for you to... 'think about it,'" he said, opening the door to reveal a set of stairs going down. Roy had been lucky enough to haggle a bargain deal for his building five years ago, before it got demolished like so many of the others in the area.

I rolled my eyes and headed downstairs. I reached another closed door at the bottom of the stairs, and gave a small knock. "Cheryl? Alex? It's me, Tootsie."

The door opened a crack, and Cheryl appeared. "Hey." She stepped aside and let me in.

I entered the ambient-lit mid-sized room. Roy had a swell setup after converting the old speakeasy into a cozy guest pad. My feet sank into the soft fiery-orange shag carpet. His flashy taste in decorating went beyond his fashion sense.

"I'm making a drink. Want one?" Cheryl asked, heading to the minibar.

"No, thanks." I approached the leather couch, where Alex lay holding a cold compress on his forehead. A notable black-and-blue mark surrounded his left eye. He looked up at me and frowned.

"Hey, Alex." I gave him a nervous smile. "Uh, how are you feeling?"

Alex groaned and closed his eyes.

"He's all right," Cheryl said from behind me.

I looked up at Cheryl's reflection in the large mirror hanging on the wood paneling behind the couch. Cupping a glass of liquor in her hands, she approached me.

"He's got a splitting headache," Cheryl continued. "Your boyfriend's got some punch on him. Maybe he oughtta take up boxing."

I turned. "Been there, done that. It ain't his bag."

"Shame." Concern swept through Cheryl's big brown eyes. "Did you find Lu?"

I shook my head. "Not yet, but I got some more clues after I left your place."

She sank onto the arm of the couch and frowned as I filled her in on my adventures in Hunt's Point. Finally, when I finished, she said, "I can't believe that Curt guy was a creep. He seemed straight when we met him at the gym. Why would he send Lu out on a bogus trip like that?"

I shrugged. "I'm thinking that my suspicions are true, in that he thought Lu and Darin were a couple." I tapped my chin. "Do you remember if the guy had a funny walk?"

"Uh… No, I don't think so. He seemed to walk pretty fine to me."

I pulled my case book from my trench coat pocket and reviewed my notes. Mel—Curt's henchman, Mr. Brown—had a slight limp. It seemed he and Curt were working together with Lu's kidnapping. *And they were planning to kill her.* I sighed and put away my book.

"What is it?" Cheryl asked with a furrowed brow.

"I'm pretty confident about who the suspects might be and that they got the wrong girl. I don't know where they would have taken Lu, but last time I encountered the suspects, they mentioned something about 'smoking a broad.'"

Cheryl gaped. "Y-You mean..."

I held up my hand to silence her. "I'm not jumping to any conclusions just yet. My next priority is to find Limpy and his boss."

Cheryl nodded slightly then gulped her drink. "I hope Darin found my message."

"What message?"

"Before we all left my apartment, I left a note for him in my bedroom, letting him know that I was okay and where I was staying."

I blinked. "You *what?*"

Cheryl looked at me, surprised. "After what you told me before about what was going on, I didn't want Darin out there worrying about me, possibly getting himself in trouble."

"Great. And what if the wrong people break into your apartment looking for you and find that note?"

"Hey, I didn't know what else to do, all right? I just want to see Darin again."

I deflated with a sigh. "Right. Well, there's nothing we can do about that now, so let's just hope, for your sake, we don't get any unwanted visitors here."

"So, what now? You don't know where Lu or Darin are, and Alex and I are trapped down here like rats for hell knows how long."

I tapped my temple as I began devising a plan. If Luanda was dead, then Curt wouldn't have much bargaining power against Darin, especially if he didn't know that Darin really loved Cheryl. Assuming Darin was still on the loose, Curt would be a dead man if Darin ever got his hands on him. Or maybe Curt *wanted* Darin to find him, and all of this could be one big trap for the unknowing boxing champion. "The guy you and Lu saw at the gym, the one who sent Lu to the cleaners, have you always seen him there at the gym?"

"Curt Zanetti..." Alex groaned.

"Huh?" I looked over my shoulder.

He rubbed his temple with his fingers. "His name..."

So it's the same guy. I turned to the couch. "You know anything else about him?"

"Nah..." Creases appeared across his brow, and his face contorted with pain. "Darin didn't... tell me much... But I almost always see Curt... hanging out all day at the gym."

"You never talked to him?"

"Never had a reason to... Only recently did I find out Darin was... working with him."

I blinked. "Why would Darin keep that information from you? I mean, you're his trainer and friend, right?"

Alex groaned. "He said he had someone promoting him... didn't go into details... I didn't think much of it, honestly. I was just... concentrating on getting him ready for the fight... I don't give two shits about the politics and business side of things."

"Hmm. Really. Now that gives me a swell idea."

"What are you going to do?" Cheryl asked.

"I'm gonna meet Curt at the gym as soon as it opens."

"What! That guy's obviously dangerous."

"So am I."

She bit her bottom lip. "Come back in one piece. And I hope the next time I see you, Darin and Lu are with you."

"I can't promise that. But will you two promise me you'll stay here until all of this is over?"

Cheryl flicked her gaze at Alex, who rolled over on his side, turning his back to us. "Yeah, sure," she said.

I left the room and headed back upstairs. Roy was no longer in his office, so I returned to the main lounge, which was ear-ringingly silent and devoid of patrons. The employees had also left, including Collins and Mitts. Roy sat alone at the bar, slouched over in his stool, nursing a drink. After over a full day of action, fatigue was starting to set in. I was half-tempted to leave Roy to wallow, but a niggling feeling gnawed at me. I supposed I could humor him for a little while before I headed home and tried to catch a few winks. I was halfway across the room when Roy suddenly lifted his head and looked toward me. He scrambled off his stool and steadied awkwardly on his feet.

"You ready to talk now?" he asked.

I sighed. *What am I about to get myself into?* "Five minutes."

His face lit up. "Right on." He brushed off the seat to his right and gestured for me to sit.

I glanced at the empty seat then, grinning coyly, planted myself on the seat to his left. I needed a bit of amusement after the previous hours' worth of rollercoaster emotions.

He huffed. "You did that on purpose."

"Did not. I like this seat better."

"Whatever." He headed behind the bar and began preparing a drink. "Look, I'm worried about you. The news is so depressing lately. Crime, murders, kidnappings… I don't know what I would do if I ever lost you."

I slumped over, resting my elbow on the bar, my cheek cradled in my palm. "You'll be fine, Roy."

He stopped pouring liquor from a bottle and glared at me. "You think I'm joking? Don't you care about my feelings?"

"Of course I care. But you're getting stressed over nothing. Besides, you've got plenty of bombshells out there for your choosing."

"I don't *want* a bombshell. I want you."

I arched an eyebrow.

"I just wish you wouldn't be so damned stubborn." He mixed the contents in a shaker then transferred it to a tall glass with ice.

"Hey, I'm a professional, Roy. Business before pleasure."

"Your problem is too much business and not enough pleasure." He slid the glass to me. "Drink that."

I looked at the glass's light, frothy contents. "What is it? A milkshake?"

"No, I call it a Tootsie Roll Cocktail."

I was tempted to take a sip but reluctantly resisted the urge. "You know I don't drink while I'm working."

"Oh, for crying out loud. You don't drink, don't smoke—hell, I don't even think I've ever heard you curse. Maybe you should've joined a convent."

I chuckled. "Nah, not my style."

"Neither is this dangerous detective life you've gotten yourself into. When are you gonna finally settle down, huh?"

I shrugged. "When there's no more crime to be had in this city."

"You're kidding, right? You're almost thirty, beautiful, no husband, no children. How long are you gonna wait to finally change all that?"

I wrinkled my nose. "Who says I want to change anything?"

"I think you've been watching too much *Mary Tyler Moore*."

"Has it ever occurred to you that maybe I actually *like* what I do?"

"Yeah? And what are you going to do when you're too old to be a detective, huh?"

I grinned. "You're never too old to solve a mystery."

He rolled his eyes. "Somehow, I knew you'd say that. Seriously, though. You need to take a break from your wild-goose chase and live a little. Trust me."

I hated to admit it, but he was probably right. With Luanda's trail going cold, I wouldn't be able to put my second plan into motion until later that morning. I finally swiped up the glass and sniffed the drink. It smelled like Roy really laid on more alcohol than I cared for. I was a lightweight, anyway.

I took a small sip. As the smooth contents slid down my throat, I perked up a little. The familiar taste of Tootsie Rolls lingered on my tongue. Strangely, I could barely taste the alcohol. *Hmm. Is it one of those 'sneaky' drinks?* I wondered.

"You like it?" Roy asked.

I took another long sip. "It's good. It kinda does taste like a Tootsie Roll."

"Told ya."

"What's in it?"

"Creme de cacao, chocolate liqueur, and light cream. They make magic together."

I drank about half and would've downed it all, but I stopped when a slight tipsy feeling hit me. I pushed the glass aside. "No more. I need my brain ready to get back to work later."

Smiling, he pulled the glass in front of himself. "So, is this the only way I'm ever gonna be able to spend time with you? Loading you up on Tootsie Roll cocktails and chatting about your work stuff?"

I gave him a skeptical look as he polished off the rest of my drink. "Maybe. But you never cared about my 'work stuff' before, so why does it matter to you?"

"If it means sharing rare moments like these with you, then it matters everything to me."

Groaning, I slid off my stool. "Look, I'm going home to try and get a quick nap in. Need to be awake again in a few hours."

He zipped from around the counter. "Wait. Let me drive you home."

I snorted, thinking about his rusty fourteen-year-old Corvair that miraculously still ran but had more problems than it was worth. "You're not driving me anywhere in that beat-up hunk of junk."

"Hey, it runs just fine."

"When are you going to finally get rid of that thing and get a new car? You seem to be making some good bread around here to afford something better."

His eyes widened. "Are you kidding? I ain't getting a new car only to have it stripped down to its axles the next day. My Corvair is surviving the times just fine."

"Yeah, even the car thieves know that jalopy ain't worth its weight in parts."

He bristled.

"I'm going to call a cab," I said.

"When are we gonna be able to do this again?"

I shrugged. "I dunno. Maybe when this case is closed."

"But…" He paused then took my hands in his.

I tensed. His touch was gentle, soft, and warm. His were hands that were best spent exploring one of the many delicate buxom brunettes that frequented this bar, instead of a rough-and-tumble girl from the street.

His Adam's apple bobbed, and his gaze faltered from mine for a moment, as if he were thinking of the right words to say. For his sake, it had better not be a marriage proposal. I kept my hawk gaze on his knees, looking for the slightest signs of bending.

"Roy..." I warned.

He swallowed again. "I can't believe I'm saying this, but..." He squeezed my hands. "I want to help you—with your case."

I blinked several times. Surely, my ears were deceiving me. "Say what?"

"Mitts gave me the lowdown while you were downstairs. You guys practically drove all over the city looking for that missing woman. Well, save your cab fare. Let me drive you around instead."

"Don't you have a business to run?"

"I have a manager, y'know. I can afford to take time off to help you."

"Why do you want to get involved with my work all of a sudden?"

He squeezed my hands again. "Because I care about you. I'm tired of only being able to see you once in a blue moon. So if this is the only way I can spend more time with you, then so be it."

I yanked my hands away. "If you really care about me, then you would let me do this my own way."

His gaze dulled. "'Your way' is liable to get you killed, especially these days. You can't save the world."

"No, but I'll do what I can to make it a little better."

"C'mon, Tootsie. You can still do your work. I'll just drive. What's the harm in that?"

I pursed my lips. Saving cab fare was always nice, but having to endure Roy's corny jive talking was not. But Roy was stubborn. I daresay, as stubborn as me. I guessed that was one thing we had in common. I deflated with a huge sigh. "Fine. Eight a.m. My place. Don't be late."

CHAPTER 9

The obnoxious ringing of the telephone next to my futon jolted me awake. Groaning, I groped around for the receiver then dragged it to my ear. "Detective Carter speaking..." I slurred.

"Tootsie. Glad you're awake," Chief Lewis said, amusement in his voice.

I let out a huge sigh. "Ugh. C'mon, Chief. I just got to sleep." I rolled over and glanced at the flip-clock radio. 7:04. I perked up. *Wow, three hours goes by fast.* "Or not."

"Well, y'know, I'm just paying you back for waking me up at two in the morning to give me that ten-twenty-four report."

"You'd rather I'd just left the old man's corpse there?"

"Nah, you're fine. The boys got things taken care of out there. Anyway, I have that information you asked for."

I rubbed the sleep from my eyes and scooted myself up on the pillow a little. "What information?"

"Damn, you really must've had a long night. Don't you remember calling me again three hours ago? About the name lookup?"

Yawning, I glanced toward the window. Dark-blue light from the early-morning sky filtered in between the slats of the closed blinds. "Oh yeah… Curt What's-His-Face…" I mumbled, finally remembering phoning the chief before plopping into bed.

"Zanetti," the chief corrected. "I had Jim, the records clerk, come in an hour early to look him up in the files."

I sat all the way up, fully awake. "Whatcha got?"

"Pretty interesting, actually. Back in '68, he was indicted for fraud and got out on bail. Couple of years later, he was arrested for involvement in some racketeering activity, which had alleged loose connections with an organized crime syndicate. But there wasn't enough evidence to put him away. He'd been off the radar ever since."

I blinked several times. "What kind of crime syndicate are we talking here? Mafia-level? 'Cause I ain't a G-man."

"Nah, I don't think so. Else we wouldn't have closed the case on him. Pretty sure it was a much smaller group. Still, small ones grow into big ones, especially when they don't have cops breathing down their backs. If you got something on Curt, we can bring him in and maybe find out where the rest of his rat friends are hiding."

"I'm not sure if Curt is working with an organization or if he's riding solo. Anything on his lackey, Mel?"

"Not much. His name is Melvin Beasley, a second-rate con man, with a couple of petty theft charges. Nothing substantial."

I sighed. "Well, ain't that helpful."

"If you learn something new, let me know."

"Oh, don't worry. You'll hear from me again real soon."

"Good. And for the love of Saint Mary, please be careful out there."

I smiled. Always like the protective big brother, he was. "You got it. Later, Chief."

I hung up the telephone and slid out of bed. I had less than an hour to get ready before Roy showed up. After a quick shower and getting dressed, I fixed a bowl of instant oatmeal. It would be enough to hold me over until lunchtime. I wasn't anticipating hanging out at the gym for too long, but then again, I was going out on a limb thinking Curt would show his face around there today.

Around ten till eight, the telephone rang again. I answered to Roy's confused voice on the other end. I blinked. "Roy? You realize you have less than ten minutes to get your butt over here?"

"Sorry, Tootsie, but, uh… you need to come to the bar. Now."

I blinked again. "What? Why? What's going on?"

"You tell me. As I left the bar to head out your way, I was stopped by this man. He started asking me questions."

"What man? What questions?"

Roy sighed. "Look, I can't talk anymore. This guy's giving me the stare-down, and I don't need him making a mess of my bar. Just get over here, will you?"

"I'll be right there." Hanging up the telephone, I felt my chest tighten. Was Roy in trouble? Had Curt and his gang found out where Cheryl was hiding? There was no time to lose. I dialed the cab company and asked for Sid, but his shift didn't start for another two hours. I would have to take what I could get at this point.

I raced to the front door, grabbed my hat and coat off the rack, and slipped them on. As I opened the door, the pungent, musty odor of skunk and ash socked my senses. Apparently, Beth, my next-door neighbor was out and about with her usual early-morning ritual. Every morning when she woke up, she indulged in her pot, which she'd described as "lighting up a new day of hope and happiness." Well, all that hope and happiness not only emanated from her clothes but also seeped out of her apartment and into the hallway. A stink like no other.

Dressed in a loose white chiffon top and a long, flowing, paisley-printed gypsy skirt, Beth stood barefoot on a stepstool and unhooked a sprig of dill herb hanging over her door. Beth was an interesting—to put it mildly—middle-aged woman. She owned a head shop and dabbled in what she called "mystical magic" that somehow, according to her, "kept her frozen in the universe of time." Strangely enough, I was inclined to believe her. It was like she'd never left the Summer of Love, spewing old news and staying forever young in her outrageous, eclectic thoughts and mannerisms. But despite it all, she was harmless.

Humming a tune, she pulled out a fresh herb sprig from one of the front pockets of her skirt. Like every other morning, she tied the sprig with twine and secured it over her door. She'd once told me it was "evil eye repellent" to keep the bad spirits away. Maybe there was something to that ritual, because despite all the building's attempted robberies, her little shop remained untouched. Then again, so was my place, but I always figured that was because we were fortunate to have smart robbers who knew better than to break into a private eye's office.

I held my breath, but it didn't take away the initial memory of the cannabis smell that clung to my nose. The headache-inducing stench would have made Pepé Le Pew jealous. Back then, while my peers were busy having fun getting high, I was working my way through the police academy— always the square, my party-heavy peers had often said. But Dick Tracy, my childhood hero, always kept his nose clean, so I felt obligated to do the same. Funny how things turned out.

I locked my office door, and as I was about to head down the hallway, Beth whipped her head to me, her waist-length braid swishing like a horse's tail.

"Ah, Tootsie. The universe greets you." She climbed down the stepstool and approached me. "Will you be joining me for the protests today?"

I exhaled then staggered my breathing. "Uh, no. I'm in a bit of a hurry. What protest is going on now?" Honestly, it seemed like a day didn't go by when there wasn't some kind of march or protest happening downtown.

Beth looked at me as if I were from another planet. "The war, of course. We must make our voices heard. We cannot stand by and let this go on anymore."

I wrinkled my nose. "Um, the war is pretty much over."

"That's what The Man wants you to think."

"Right… well… look. Sorry, I can't join you on your protest. I have some important business to take care—"

"This is a matter of our freedom, Tootsie. Our very existence. The universe is not pleased with what has happened. We must all do our part in this moment of solidarity."

"I am doing my part, Beth. I'm trying to stop some bad people. I'm helping to make the world a better place, aren't I?"

She looked thoughtful for a moment then smiled softly. "Ah, I suppose you are." She assessed me from head to toe then extended her hands. "Come. Show me your hands. I must know what is in store for you today."

I cleared my throat, trying to stave off the overpowering sensation of her "happy perfume." "I really don't have time to—"

"Don't argue! The universe demands your safety."

Groaning, I stuck out my hands. She examined both sides of my palms then traced her index finger along the lines. Her face suddenly turned somber. "Oh dear..."

"What?"

"Today is not a good day for you to go out. You will face a loss of a life."

"Yeah, if you don't let me get going, someone may die. This is... uh, police business. Yeah, that's it. Official police business, so I need to leave now before—"

"It's inevitable. If you leave this building, breathe the air outside, a dark aura will surround you, and you will be a magnet for death."

I pulled my hands away. "Well, I'm no stranger to death. And the air outside ain't clean anyway, so I'm sure I'll be a magnet for a lot of things."

She shook her head solemnly. "Please heed my warning, Tootsie. Don't leave. You are a bright, shining star that is destined to do great things someday. Maybe you'll be a peacemaker, like Dr. King. Have you seen and heard all the great things he's been doing?" She clapped her hands together and grinned. "Oh, I hope he makes time to come here and speak soon. If anyone can get the people riled up about ending this damned war, he can."

"You realize Dr. King is..." I rolled my eyes. "Never mind. Sorry, Beth. I need to go."

"Oh, Tootsie... May the universe spare your poor, lost soul..."

I'd never been happier to be outside, breathing in the smoggy morning air. Unfortunately, the hippie weed still lingered on my clothes like a bad dream. A Checker cab was waiting along the curb. I jumped in, and we zipped to Queens as fast as the rush-hour traffic would allow.

Finally reaching Kronos Lounge thirty minutes later, I paid the fare and hopped out. The building's exterior looked bare and abandoned—much different than it did at night. I jogged through an alley to the back of the building, where Roy's beat-up red Corvair was parked, its rusted front bumper barely hanging on by a few bolts. I approached the lounge's back door, discovered it locked, then pounded on it with my fist. "Open up, Roy! It's me!"

I waited a few moments, but there was no answer. I pounded again a few more times, but it was useless. He must've been down in the speakeasy or upstairs in his apartment, where he couldn't hear me. At least, I hoped that was the case. Roy had sounded nervous on the telephone, more nervous than usual. I didn't want to believe that Curt and his goons might've discovered this place. The faint, lingering scent of Beth's perfume reminded me of her foreboding fortune-telling. My throat tightened. *"A loss of life..."* No... *it couldn't be Roy... could it? Not Roy!*

I looked up at the second-story window, which was the kitchen to Roy's apartment. The window was shut, but getting inside didn't look like it would be too difficult, thanks to the age of this building. I found a small metal wedge next to a covered dumpster and stuffed it in my coat pocket. Then I rolled the dumpster under the hinged ladder of the fire escape. I climbed onto the dumpster and jumped, grabbing the metal ladder. I'd remembered the days of doing this as a kid, trying to spy on the neighbors while I practiced my Dick Tracy sleuthing skills. As I maneuvered my way to the opposite end, the ladder's hinges yielded to my weight and levered downward with a noisy creak. I climbed around and hurried up the stairs.

Reaching the window, I pulled the metal wedge from my pocket. The old wooden frame had fallen victim to the elements. Peeking inside, I saw the tarnished sash lock was in its secure position, but the one screw that held it down was halfway out. I peered further into the room to see if anyone was there, but the place looked empty. I stuck the wedge under the bottom of the window frame and jiggled it a few times. The latch wobbled with my movements. I gave the wedge another firm shove upward, and the lock broke, flailing on its lone, wobbly screw like a flag. I tossed the wedge away and pushed the window the rest of the way up with my hands.

Climbing inside, I glanced around the bare kitchen and listened for sounds. It was quieter than the public library. My heart pounded. I had half a mind to call out to Roy, but that would give me away if Curt was here. I pulled out my gun and quietly searched each of the rooms. Roy's obnoxious taste in interior decoration continued in his apartment, far worse than the speakeasy. This place was the definition of a shag pad. At last, I reached his bedroom. A massive, king-sized waterbed sat prominently on a raised, red-carpeted platform. Roy had proudly dubbed this place the Red Room of Satisfaction, for reasons other than because it looked like someone had been murdered so their blood could be used to paint the furniture, ceiling, walls, and ankle-deep shag carpet.

I'd only entered his room a few times, and thankfully, it was never to "get satisfied." But Roy knew better than to think that I was another one of his mindless dames. Amid the sanguine-hued heaven, something gold sat on his nightstand—a framed picture of him and me from New Year's in '72. It was one of the few pictures of us that I actually liked, but the thought of it sitting in this room made my toes curl. How many other women had come in here and seen that picture while they were in the height of their... moment? Obviously, Roy had no shame.

I left the bedroom in a hurry, my eyes still aching from all the red-hued everything. With his apartment thoroughly searched, I left through the front door and headed downstairs. The bar was quiet and empty. That left only one place to check. Tightening my grip on my gun, I silently approached Roy's closed office door and eased my ear against it. All was quiet. I tried the knob. It was unlocked. Sucking in a breath, I made my way inside. The office was empty, but the door leading down to the speakeasy was wide open. Approaching the stairs, I began to hear several muffled voices. One of them, a man's I didn't recognize, sounded heated. Another was Roy's, shrill and stammering two octaves higher. I'd known Roy all my life, and rarely, if ever, was he intimidated by other people. Whoever this mysterious stranger was, he meant business. Or maybe I was about to walk in on a certain death. I swallowed a lump in my throat, readied my gun, and padded down the stairs.

"I'm tired of waiting. That broad better get here, or else!" the mysterious male voice growled.

"H-Hey, man, she's coming, I swear. Don't do nothing crazy, all right?" Roy stammered.

"I want answers, and I want 'em *now*!"

"Hey, easy. Easy. Put him down," Alex said calmly.

Taking a deep breath, I rested my hand on the closed door of the speakeasy. Slowly and silently, I turned the knob. As the door crept open, I spotted the back of a man I didn't recognize holding Roy up with a fistful of his shirt collar. His other hand was cocked back. Roy's eyes were bugged out, and his face was ghostly white.

Oh no! Roy!

I exhaled and flung open the door. "Hold it!" I barked, aiming my gun at the stranger's back.

A hush fell over the room. Cheryl huddled herself to the side, her hands clasped over her mouth while she looked on at the fight, wide-eyed. Alex held his arms out to break up the two men. Alex looked at me and gawked.

The stranger turned around, did a double take, and slowly released Roy, raising his hands in surrender.

The man was Darin Rivers.

CHAPTER 10

I wasn't sure whether to be relieved or shocked to find Darin here. I lowered my gun and cautiously slid it back into my coat. Darin's body stiffened. He came off as the ticking-time-bomb type, and I preferred not to get the champion boxer any more riled up than he seemed to be already. Roy was still quivering, but thankfully, he was unharmed.

"Tootsie! Holy cow, am I glad to see you!" Roy exclaimed, panting in relief.

"What's going on here?" I demanded, my gaze swiveling from Roy to Darin, Cheryl, then Alex.

Darin marched over to me and glowered. "You the detective looking for Lu?"

I tilted my head up slightly, gawking at Darin's solid frame. He sure looked a lot bigger up close than he had in the ring from a distance. His hands, scarred and calloused, had seen their share of battles. Darin was slightly shorter and less bulky than Mitts, but he appeared just as menacing. Still, Mitts had him beat by a few dozen pounds of muscle and a couple more inches.

I bet Mitts would give Darin a run for his money. That was one fight I would love to see. I cleared my throat, attempting to calm my nerves. "That's right. Have you seen her?"

"No."

"How did you know about this place?"

Darin cast a glance at Cheryl then looked back at me. "I went by Cheryl's place earlier and found her note."

I rubbed my hand down my face in exasperation. "Did anyone see you come here?"

He shrugged. "How the hell should I know? Cheryl's apartment was a mess. Her door was broken, and I assumed the worst. I found her note in her bedroom and came straight here. After that threat Curt made, I—"

"What threat?" I raised my eyebrows.

"The one about him hurting my woman if I didn't throw the match. I thought he was straight before, but it turned out he was up to something. I wasn't about to lose to that punk Wesson, so I had to do what I had to do and get the hell out of there fast before Curt followed through with his threat."

I tapped my chin. *So, Curt was intending to hurt Lu, thinking she was Darin's girlfriend. But Darin thought Curt was going to hurt Cheryl instead.*

Cheryl edged closer to us. "I don't think he or his friends were ever going to come. They took Lu instead."

"Yeah…" Darin scowled. "And I'm gonna kill that son of a bitch."

"Whoa. Hold on." I held up my hands. "Do you know where Curt and his gang might be holding Lu?"

Darin sneered. "If I knew that, I wouldn't be here, now would I?"

Grimacing, I scratched the side of my jaw. "No, I suppose not."

"Look, you're the detective. Aren't you supposed to figure these things out?"

"Well, I can't do much without information. Tell me exactly what Curt said to you before your match last night."

As Darin opened his mouth to reply, Alex headed to the telephone on a side table in the bar area and picked up the receiver.

I held up my index finger. "Excuse me, Alex. Who are you about to call?"

Alex grunted, flicking his gaze in my direction. "That's none of your business, missy."

Roy bowed up to him, scowling. "Hey, show her some respect."

"Easy, Roy," I said, resisting the urge to roll my eyes. Alex was not only a few inches taller than Roy but also hefty enough to smash poor Roy into a pancake. "Look," I said to Alex. "There are some guys out there after your fighter." I stuck my thumb at Darin. "They might have this place bugged. The telephones might be tapped. Or they might be staking out this bar right now as we speak."

Alex gripped the receiver. "Ain't nothing I gotta say that they'll care about."

Darin's jaw clenched. His body tensed. "I hope those bastards are staking out this place. Makes my job easier in busting their skulls." He smacked his fist into his hand and cracked his knuckles a few times.

"No!" I held my hand up at the headstrong fighter. "Not yet, anyway. I have reason to believe the suspects might be involved in an organized crime syndicate. That's bad news, y'dig? They have numbers, most likely guns, and leverage. We have to go about this carefully if we're going to get Lu back safely."

"She's right," Cheryl said, wrapping her arm around Darin's and resting her head on his shoulder.

"Please, baby, just calm down and let her handle it." She caressed his arm.

Darin's body relaxed slowly. "Fine," he grumbled. "We'll do it your way, Detective."

"Good." I turned back to Alex. "Now, I'm going to ask again. Who are you calling?"

The trainer's left eye twitched. "If you must know, I'm calling Primo Deluca, the owner at Primo's Boxing Club, to see if he can hold one of the rings for us for the day."

I blinked. "You're not thinking about training at a time like this, are you?"

"I'm not, but he is." Alex nodded to Darin.

Darin rolled his eyes. "C'mon, man. Last night was rough."

"Damn right, it was. That's why you're gonna get your ass to the gym and train. It's for your own good."

"But Lu…"

Alex pointed his finger at me. "That's *her* department, not yours."

"I would highly advise you both to not leave this place for the time being," I said.

Alex's eyebrow arched. "There's no sense in us waiting around, twiddling our thumbs, when Darin has work to do."

"Yes, but—"

"This is *your* case, ain't it, *Detective?*"

"Yes, but—"

"Then I suggest you do your damn job."

I sighed. They weren't making solving this case any easier.

Frowning, Roy watched Alex stab the buttons with his finger. Alex turned his back to us and leaned against the minibar counter as he held the receiver to his ear.

"Hey," Darin muttered to us in a volume that was out of Alex's earshot. "Don't take it the wrong way, Detective. He's just as pissed about all this as I am, if not more. He's been in this game longer than me, and even he didn't see this coming. Curt is one slick mother."

"Doesn't he care that Curt has put a target out on you?"

"Of course he cares. Alex has been salty as hell about it."

"All right," I said. "Let's start over. What exactly did Curt say to you last night before your match?"

Darin's gaze flicked toward Alex then to me, and he sighed. "He said there was a lot of money riding on this fight and that 'I better come through and throw the fight, or he's going to pay a visit to my girl.'"

I raised my eyebrows. "'Your girl,' meaning Cheryl?"

Cheryl bit her lip, her gaze bouncing between us.

He nodded. "It completely took me by surprise. I've been with him for about three months now. He knew I was trying to make a comeback and saw I was struggling to get fights, so he picked me up as his sort-of-manager-promoter guy. He told me to keep the arrangement under wraps for the time being. I didn't think much about that, especially since he got me fights left and right. Three fights a week sometimes. It was like Christmas."

"Alex didn't know anything about this?" I asked.

Darin shook his head. "Nope. I just told him I signed my name up to a bunch of events. I never mentioned Curt. Alex doesn't care about the politics or business side of things." Darin looked sidelong at his friend, who was still on the telephone, then turned to me and lowered his voice even more. "He just likes being a damned drill sergeant to me."

Cheryl let out an airy chuckle. "That just means he cares, baby."

"What happened next?" I urged Darin.

"Well, the morning before the fight, Curt and I talked. He stressed about how important this fight was and that in order for me to ensure my comeback, I would need to take a dive."

I furrowed my brow. "I don't understand that logic."

Darin shrugged. "According to Curt, I was winning too much. He said I had to slow down a bit. I don't know what he was talking about. I felt like I got lucky in some of those fights."

"But you still won them, right?"

"Yeah, but barely. Some of those fights were plenty tough. A few, I won by points. Others, I managed to get the KO. And yeah, some guys I fought were pushovers, but I guess I had the luck of the draw. But a win is a win, right?" He shrugged.

"Did you know any of the fighters?"

"Nope. Not one. Curt said they were from out of state. But I liked that, y'know? It really put my skills to the test. Alex was cool with it too."

I nodded slightly. Smart on Curt's part to bring in non-local fighters so no one would get suspicious—an easy way for this arrangement to look like fair and challenging fights.

"Everything seemed legit, until last night, when I was expected to throw the fight. That bothered me, y'know? I got my pride and dignity. Curt told me to think about it, but I already made up my mind. Before the fight, while Alex and I were alone in the locker room, I told Alex everything and what I planned to do. He wasn't cool with it, but he went along with the plan anyway. After the third round, he snuck out of the arena and headed to Cheryl's like I'd told him. Meanwhile, I stretched the rest of the fight for as long as I could to give him time to head over there before Curt or his friends did."

I rubbed my chin. "I see. So that explains why I found Alex and Cheryl together."

Darin nodded.

"Seems to be a case of mistaken identity on Curt's part. Either way, Luanda is still in trouble. You took a big gamble, Darin."

Darin shrugged. "How the hell was I supposed to know he was gonna take Lu?"

"He's taken his con game to the next level."

"What!" Alex spun around. His eyes widened as he white-knuckled the receiver at his ear.

I looked up at the tone of terror in the trainer's voice.

"Is he there now?" Alex asked. His gaze darted around the room then settled on Darin. "Well, you tell that son of a bitch to lay off, or he'll get what's comin' to him." He slammed the receiver on the cradle and ran his hands through his thick hair.

"Problems?" I called.

Alex glared. "Some wiseguy stopped at the gym to give Primo a message."

"What kind of message?"

Alex returned to us. "For Darin. He said something about Darin being 'due to pay in full.' Some 'arrangement' has been made, and Darin's going to be picked up at the gym at one p.m. sharp.

And he better be there, or his career will be over for good."

"That's a little over four hours from now," Darin said.

"It's obviously a trap," I said flatly.

Darin rubbed the back of his head. "I know. I owe Curt money for not throwing that fight. Last night's winnings will barely make a dent. I don't know what he's gonna want me to do…"

"Did they happen to say where they were intending to take Darin?" I asked Alex.

Alex shook his head. "Nope."

Yeah, of course not. I rubbed my chin. It was then that I realized Curt and his friends most likely didn't know about this bar. "I think I have an idea on how I can spring a trap on the trap. I'm going to need you, Darin."

"Hell no!" Alex exclaimed. "He's gonna go train. Maybe we oughtta go back to Philly and train there instead."

Roy inched closer to Alex and crossed his arms. "Hey, man. If Tootsie says she has a plan, then listen to her, damn it. She's the smartest person in this room and Darin's best bet in getting these goons off his back."

Alex growled at him.

I slapped my forehead. Roy's chivalrous intentions were admirable, but they weren't helping this delicate situation. "Roy, now's not the time—"

"No, Tootsie. I don't like the way he talks to you."

Alex turned to Roy. "Listen, you son of a…"

Roy unfolded his arms and bowed up to him fearlessly, though it did nothing to match the other man's height and girth. "You're free to get the hell out of my bar anytime you want."

"Guys…" Cheryl called.

"Everyone, stop!" I stood between Roy and Alex and pushed them away, anticipating stray fists flying my way. Thankfully, none came. "None of you are helping right now. If you would please just listen to what I have to say…" I waited a beat. When I had everyone's attention, I continued. "First of all, I want Alex and Cheryl to stay here. Based on what Alex said from that telephone call, I have a strong suspicion that Curt and his gang don't know where Darin is, which means we can consider this place safe for now."

Cheryl nodded. "If it means getting Lu back safe and sound, I'll keep my ass here for as long as I need to."

Alex exhaled through his nose as he gave me the stink eye. "I'll stay here one day and not a day more. You follow? *One* day."

I smiled and nodded. One day was all I needed. Heck, it was all I had. "Right on."

"So, I guess I'm the bait, eh?" Darin said.

"You got it. We need to know where Curt intends to take you. I want you to already be at the gym before he comes. When they come get you, make absolutely certain you leave out the front of the building. We need to make this as casual as possible so no random bystander gets suspicious enough to call the cops."

"Cops…" Darin grimaced and rubbed the back of his head. "I'd rather not get them involved."

"Oh, they're definitely getting involved. Just not right away. First, we need to make sure Lu is returned safely. If those goons see one badge at the rendezvous point, I'm almost certain that'll be the last we'll see of them *and* Lu."

"And where are you going to be in all this, Tootsie?" Roy asked, concern in his voice.

"I'll be staking out the place, waiting for Curt's gang to show. Once he does, I'll follow him to his secret meeting spot."

"You're not doing this alone."

"I never said I was."

Roy's face brightened. "You're gonna finally let me help you?"

"Yeah. Your junkyard-quality car is perfect to hide in. It'll blend in nicely with the other beat-up, abandoned cars. Curt and his friends won't suspect a thing."

He bristled. "There's nothing wrong with my car. It runs just fine. Purrs like a kitten."

"Yeah, a kitten whose tail got smashed between a door." I rolled my eyes. "Anyway, that's the base plan. Any questions?" I looked to everyone in turn.

Roy opened his mouth to say something, then he closed it. Smart on his part. I could already sense this was going to be a long day.

We set the plan in motion. While Cheryl and Alex remained in the speakeasy, Darin took a bus over to the gym. Roy and I met in his office to discuss one other matter.

I handed Roy his desk telephone. "Call Mitts."

He wrinkled his nose as he gingerly took the black receiver from me. "Why?"

"Because I'm going to need a bit of enforcement in case things turn south."

"You don't think I'm perfectly capable of protecting you?"

I fought down an amused smile then gave him a skeptical, arched brow. "Let's just say, if I hadn't come down to the speakeasy when I did, I'd be scraping your remains off the ground by now."

Roy's mouth opened and closed, like he was fighting with himself for a logical explanation. Then he tilted his head at me curiously. "Were you worried about me?"

"What kind of question is that? Of course I was worried about you."

He beamed. "It's nice to know I have a place in your heart."

I snorted. *Yeah, a place smaller than my pinky, you turkey.* "Look, you're a good businessman. I'll give you that. But leave the street fighting to the knuckleheads." I pointed at the receiver. "Call Mitts."

Roy sulked then punched in Mitts's number. I opened one of his desk drawers and pulled out a small black case that contained his mini binoculars. "I need to borrow these," I said, slipping the case into my trench coat pocket. I swore that one of these days, I was going to get myself a better set of binoculars. Roy's was state-of-the-art and always kept in pristine condition, as if he'd barely used them. But I doubted that was the case. I didn't know a ladies' man who didn't own a pair of high-quality binoculars.

Roy covered the speaker with his hand. "Hey, those cost me a pretty penny, y'know."

"Geez Louise. I'll give them back."

"If I didn't care about you so damn much…" He grunted. "You've no idea how lucky you are to have someone like me around. You know that?"

"I wholeheartedly agree, Roy. You've no idea how lucky you are to have someone like me around." I quirked a smile at him then left the office. I scoured the rest of the bar, making sure there was nothing out of the ordinary. I figured there wouldn't be, but I checked around anyway for my own reassurance. No wire bugs, no broken windows or locks, and no other clues that could suggest this bar was no longer safe. Everything checked out as clean as a whistle.

By nine forty-five, Roy stormed out of his office, looking like he'd just sucked on a lemon.

"Well? Is he coming, or what?" I asked.

Roy shook his head. "He said he has to go on his morning jog first, then he'll come."

"What! Doesn't he realize how urgent this is?"

"I told him, but you know Mitts. He just does what he does when he feels like it. Maybe you should've talked to him instead. He might've listened to you, especially after you managed to coerce him into that cab with you last night."

"Hey, he came willingly… eventually."

"Right. Well, I told him where we'll be. One can only hope that he decides to come."

"For his sake, he'd better." I sighed, already brainstorming an alternate plan should Mitts leave us hanging, because I had a strange gut feeling that today was going to go anything but smoothly.

CHAPTER 11

Traffic never let up as Roy's jalopy crawled its way to Hunt's Point. The engine had sputtered several times, threatening to cut off, but by some miracle, that old ticker just kept on going. By ten o'clock, we were parallel parked along the curb on Whittier Street, which crossed Randall Avenue, where Primo's Boxing Club sat. A couple of old stripped cars sat in front and back of us. I had a clear view of everyone coming in and out of the gym. So far, Darin hadn't exited. Before Roy and I had left the bar, I had called Primo and instructed him to keep all doors locked, except the front entrance. There would be no way for Curt's people to get the drop on us and sneak in without my knowing. Primo was swell to cooperate—well, that is, after I kind of told him it was official police business. Technically, it was—well, it would be, soon enough.

"Y'know, you'd have more leg room if you sat up here with me," Roy said from the driver's seat.

You'd like that, wouldn't you? "No, thanks. I'm fine," I replied, not lowering the binoculars. My legs and knees were aching from the cramped backseat, and my muscles were still buzzing from the intense vibrations of the car's thunderous, rumbling engine, long after Roy had shut it off. Sitting in the front seat would not have been easier, because being that close to Roy would get distracting, if not annoying. No, I couldn't give the helpless romantic any more ammunition than he already had.

"Hey, I took a shower, y'know," Roy said. When I didn't respond, he continued, "Are we really going to be sitting here for three hours?"

"We sure are. Maybe longer. Who knows?" I lowered my binoculars and raised an eyebrow at him. "What's wrong? Bored already?"

"Well, I ain't exactly on the edge of my seat here." He flicked on the radio to a low volume. Music from his favorite jazz-funk station thrummed from the speakers.

"You're the one who wanted so desperately to join me on my case so you can 'be closer' to me.

Well, welcome to my world, where sometimes sitting in one spot for hours on end, waiting for something to happen is the exciting part of the job."

Roy wrinkled his nose. "How in the hell do you find this exciting?"

I shrugged and then returned to my stakeout. "Guess I'm weird like that." Suddenly, I was met with a big blurry image as Roy moved his face in front of the lenses. I started, yanking my face back. "Hey, you mind?"

He pulled the binoculars away. "I was thinking. After this case is over, I want to take you out to dinner."

"After this case is over, I'm going to be too tired to go out anywhere."

"Okay, then. I'll make you dinner. You can stay at my place."

I snorted. "First of all, you can't cook. And second, if you think for a second I'm going to sleep in your shag-motel apartment…"

"Hey, you're the only woman allowed in my apartment."

"You're a terrible liar. Your apartment is too fancy to enjoy alone."

"Well, it's true, you know. And for your information, I can too cook." He lifted his head proudly. "I made spaghetti last night, and it was perfect."

I couldn't tell whether he was being serious or facetious, but the idea of Roy trying to find his way around the kitchen was amusing in itself. Though, I had to admit, he did make great drinks. All I could say was "I'm sure it was."

He pouted. "You don't believe me."

"Oh, I didn't say that."

"All right. So it's settled. You'll come over and have dinner with me."

I fought down a smile. Never had I ever met a man so persistent. Especially when that same man used to be the annoying little boy on the block who hated girls like the plague. "I'll think about it. Now may I *please* get back to my work?" I held out my hand for the binoculars.

He cracked a smile and gave them back. "Eight o'clock will be perfect." He nestled more comfortably in the driver's seat and closed his eyes.

I blinked. "Did you not hear what I said?"

He smirked. "Yeah. You didn't say no."

Slick. Real slick.

Two uneventful hours ticked by. Mitts still hadn't shown up, and I figured he wasn't coming at all. It baffled me that he would miss out on a potential fight. By half past noon, I'd decided it was time to check in with Chief Lewis. I reached under the front seats and groped around, snagging paperclips, crumpled slips of paper, and balls of lint.

"Got a dime?" I asked Roy.

Roy furrowed his brow. "Calling Mitts?"

"I'm done with Mitts. I need to call the chief."

"I thought you said you weren't getting cops involved?"

"I'm not—yet." I pulled my empty hand from under the seats. "Look, you got a dime, or what?"

Rolling his eyes, he pulled one out of his pocket. As I was about to take it, he held it up slightly. "Kiss me for it?"

I grunted and pulled away from him. "Don't push your luck." I opened the back door. "I'll call collect."

"All right. Fine. Here." He shoved the dime at me as I swiveled my legs out of the car.

I was still annoyed at him, but I took his dime anyway. I headed over to the nearby telephone booth and slipped inside, carefully avoiding a foul-smelling puddle of yellow liquid near my feet. I wedged the door open to let in the fresh air, but it didn't help much. I quickly dialed the chief's personal office number.

"Tootsie, where are you?" Chief Lewis asked with deep concern in his voice.

"Hunt's Point." I filled him in on the details while I kept one eye on the passersby and another on the gym's entrance in the distance. "Think you can spare a couple of your boys in a bit?"

"Yeah, sure. Trevor and Joel are heading out to a ten-thirty-nine, but I'll keep Andrew and Lenny on standby. Just say the word. One p.m., right?"

"That's what they said."

There was a brief pause. "Listen, Tootsie, and listen good. Don't go and be a hero, all right? Curt might have outside help, and you could be caught in the crossfire. You call me the *second* you see him leave that gym. Got it?"

"No can do, Chief. I have no idea where they're going. I'll have to call you again when I get to the meeting place."

He let out a deep sigh. "Damn it, Tootsie. I'll never forgive myself if anything happens to you…"

"Don't worry. I'll be careful. Promise." I ended the call and cut out of the booth. There was still no activity at the gym, so I returned to the car. As I reached for the door's handle, I started. The passenger's seat was now occupied. *Mitts?*

He took a hefty bite out of a jumbo-sized submarine sandwich, met my gaze, and waved with an awkward, cheek-bulging smile.

Geez Louise! I couldn't believe that big lug had actually come through! I squeezed into the backseat, the pungent odor of onions and salami wafting in the car's interior.

"Hey, Tootsie. Look who decided to finally show up." Roy eyed me from the rearview mirror as he propped his elbow against the door and rested his cheek in his palm.

"I told you I had stuff to do." Mitts took another bite of his sandwich.

"Yeah, yeah… And you bring all that food up in here and don't even share?" Roy motioned to the other half of the sandwich.

Mitts rolled his eyes and tore off a tiny end-piece for Roy.

"I'll pass," I said, before Mitts could offer me any. "You sure had me fooled. Didn't think you'd show up, honestly."

"Well, I'm here now, ain't I? Though it don't look like I missed much."

"Tootsie finds sitting in a car for three hours staring at a building 'exciting.' Can you believe it?" Roy said flatly.

Mitts snickered. "Yeah, I can believe it."

"You boys will never understand." A wave of anxiety began filling my body as one o'clock neared. The minutes ticked by steadily, and it seemed like an eternity. A chill traveled through my body, as if someone had dropped an ice cube down my back. I should've been used to this by now, with all my police training, but moments like these always felt like a new experience. This plan could go very well or very, very badly. I took a few deep breaths, suppressing the ugly monster called fear. *I got this.*

Mitts wolfed down the rest of his sandwich, finished it off with a bottle of root beer, and belched. "Damn, that was good."

"Sounds like it," I said, watching the gym's entrance. *One o'clock*. People came and went, but Darin didn't leave with any of them.

"For crying out loud, man. Show a little class. There's a lady present," Roy grumbled.

"Tootsie ain't a lady," Mitts said.

"He's right, Roy. I'm not a lady—not today."

"Hmph. You're always a lady in my eyes, Tootsie."

"Yeah, well, in the eyes of criminals, I'm their worst nightmare."

Mitts laughed. "For real."

1:03. I tightened my grip around the binoculars as sweat began beading on my palms. *Where are they? Or is this another set-up?* I spotted a man in a funky brown blazer approaching the entrance. I noted the slight limp in his step, which he seemed to be trying to hide. The awkward gait made him look like was trying to find the nearest restroom instead. He placed his hand on the door, paused, and looked around. His face turned in my direction. A pair of sunglasses concealed his identity but not enough to fool me. *Well, well. Hello, Mel.* "Looks like they came through," I said to Roy and Mitts as I watched Mel casually slip through the entrance. "Roy, start 'er up and get ready to go."

"They came? You sure?" Roy cranked the ignition. The engine gave a mighty lion's roar, sputtered, and groaned like a sick puppy.

"Yup." I winced from the engine's excessive vibrations that traveled from the seat and right under my rear.

"Sweet. When does the fight start?" Mitts cracked his knuckles.

"Soon," I said, not taking my eyes off the entrance. I counted the seconds. I had Primo's word that he would keep the other doors locked. I could only hope that Mel wasn't in there doing some... persuading. I gritted my teeth. *Five minutes.* I would give them five minutes before heading inside.

Two minutes later, Mel and Darin exited the gym together. I exhaled a breath I'd been inadvertently holding. Darin looked calm as he and Mel walked casually to the next street and disappeared. I caught sight of the street sign before I yanked the binoculars from my face. "They went down Bryant. Let's go, Roy!" I said.

"On it!" Roy did his usual funky shifting ritual as his hand whipped the cue ball shifter in all directions before finally settling on one position. He eased away from the curb then slammed on the gas, jolting the car forward. I braced myself. Roy performed some expert driving maneuvers, dodging incoming traffic by mere inches as he tore onto Randall Avenue and careened around the corner.

"Geez Louise! Slow down!" I barked, fumbling with the binoculars. "We're trying to be incognito here." Roy slowed to a crawl down the narrow side street. I caught Darin and Mel just in time as they piled into the back of a brown car parked ahead. "There. Brown Caprice, '70, I think."

"Looks like a '72, actually," Mitts corrected.

"Whatever." I trained the binoculars on the license plate and engrained the numbers and letters in my brain. Then I pulled my notebook from my coat pocket and jotted the sequence down.

"I see 'em," Roy said.

"Good. Stay far enough back, but keep them in your sight at all times," I instructed.

The brown car sped off, and so did we.

CHAPTER 12

The brown Caprice we were tailing crawled through the streets, as if the driver wasn't in a hurry to get to his destination. I nearly lost my sense of direction when we pulled onto the Bruckner Expressway for a short time, only to be dumped minutes later in Castle Hill. I'd had few, if any, cases out there. Not like there was much out there to begin with. The edge of town, which was lined by Westchester Creek, served as a vehicle graveyard. Abandoned cars littered empty, overgrown lots and were scattered among the rubble of destroyed buildings and garbage. Street after street bore more of the same.

The depressing scene looked like something straight out of an apocalyptic science fiction movie.

I often wondered why I decided to stay in this city with all its problems and urban decay. But the more I wondered, the more I knew I couldn't leave. *Darn it, if I wasn't stubborn.*

I hated what had become of my home, but after I'd lived here long enough, New York just sort of grew on me, and I developed a love-hate relationship. My hate for this corruption had forced me to fight for what I love, one bad guy at a time.

"Where the hell are they going?" Roy muttered as he drove, squinting at the brown Caprice far ahead. Thankfully, Roy's jalopy blended in just fine out in these parts. The driver didn't seem to pay us any mind.

"Just keep driving," I reminded him, using my binoculars to get a better view. The Caprice's brake lights flashed, and the car slowed. It turned right and disappeared through a hidden entrance beyond a graffiti-covered wooden construction wall.

"Hmm... Wonder what's through there?" Mitts asked.

"Stop the car, Roy." I craned my neck, assessing the area. We were about two hundred feet away from the entrance. I caught a glimpse of Westchester Creek and the faint, smoggy outline of the Whitestone Bridge beyond it. I took a moment to think, trying to gather my sense of direction. A couple of barely standing row homes dotted the landscape. There wasn't much in the way of people to be seen, not even junkies or gangs. It was as desolate as it came in these parts, making it the perfect incognito place for an organized crime meet-up. Several blocks ahead, beyond the construction site's perimeter, was a small area that looked less demolished than the others. I focused my binoculars ahead. The small buildings and row homes looked livable enough. I even spotted a couple of business signs—a bright-yellow one for a corner bodega, another for a pawn shop across the street. *Well, at least this place isn't* completely *deserted.* I lowered the binoculars. "There's a bodega two blocks ahead. Drive there."

"How can you think of shopping at a time like this?" Roy said.

"No questions. Just drive."

Grumbling, he put the car in gear and sped off. "I don't get why we're doing this, Tootsie. I mean, the guys are right there. This seems like a waste of time."

"I need to make sure there's no other way out of there. And just in case those guys might think we *have* been following them all this time, we can throw them off the trail." As we passed the hidden driveway, I caught a glimpse of the Caprice, another car parked beyond, and some people standing around. Before I could make out any more details, we passed a wooden wall that blocked my line of sight. Reaching the end of the perimeter, I looked out the back window. The wall extended on all sides, it seemed, stopping at the edge of the ridge that extended down to the riverbank. Satisfied with my assessment, I nestled back in my seat and smiled. "Two cars. Looks like they're trapped like rats." *Maybe Lu is somewhere near.*

"How do you figure that?" Roy arched his eyebrow.

"Just a hunch."

Arriving at the bodega, we parked along the curb, behind an abandoned, beat-up station wagon. I handed Mitts the binoculars. "Keep an eye on the construction entrance."

Taking the binoculars, Mitts scrunched his nose. "What's the plan?"

"No time to explain. I need to call the chief." I got out of the car.

"Well…" Mitts climbed out then slipped me a dime from his pocket. "I guess you got it all figured out."

"Thanks for trusting me." Grinning, I took the dime. Good on Mitts to be attentive like that. Or maybe he was just working on his gentlemanly skills. He posted himself behind Roy's car and leaned against the trunk. Roy soon joined him. I headed to the public telephone outside the bodega and dialed Chief Lewis's office as fast as the little rotary could spin. The line rang and rang. I swallowed. *Where are you, Chief?*

I rapped my fingers against the side of the telephone as the line continued ringing. "No, no, no, no, no... Not now..." I glanced toward the bodega's entrance, where people occasionally came and left. My throat tightened as I continued listening, hoping and praying that the chief would pick up. But all my efforts went unanswered. Sighing, I slowly lowered the receiver from my ear. As I was about to hang it up, I suddenly heard a faint click and a man's voice.

"Fifty-Fourth Precinct. How can I help you?" The droning voice wasn't Chief Lewis's.

I stuck the receiver back to my ear. "Hi! Put me through to Chief Robert Lewis, please!"

"He's in a meeting right now. How can I assist you, Miss?"

I blinked. "A meeting? He's expecting my call."

"Yeah, well, it was an urgent meeting. Do you need the police?"

"Yes! Uh... I mean, that is... Are Lenny and Andrew around?"

There was a pause. "Who is this?"

"My name is Tootsie."

Another pause. "You, uh... from Lillian's?"

It took me a moment to realize that he meant Lillian's Red Room, the seedy strip joint in Hunt's Point. My jaw dropped. "How dare you! I'm not a stripper!"

An older woman about to enter suddenly looked in my direction, wide-eyed and curious, then cleared her throat before shuffling inside.

"Well, whoever or whatever you are, if it's not an emergency, then please hang up," the man on the telephone said.

I rubbed my hand over my face, exasperated. "How long have you been working at that precinct?"

"'Bout four months. Why?"

I groaned. *Great.* Just my luck, I was talking to a rookie. I couldn't tip this guy off too much. He sounded like one of those by-the-book rookies who wouldn't hesitate to turn me in for using police resources like this. He was probably another one of those dirtbags who thought women belonged in bed or behind a stove and not in law enforcement. Not that I would be surprised. "I need you to give the chief a message for me, ASAP. Tell him to meet me near Zerega and Norton Avenue by the construction site."

"Look, it ain't none of my business what you two do alone. But Chief Lewis is working now and will not be disturbed."

"Please give him that message. I'm an old friend."

"Lady, you know how many prank calls we get every day from turkeys who say they're 'friends' of the chief?"

"This isn't a prank!"

"Yeah, and I'm the queen of England. Look, lady, I'm very busy right now. Don't call back here again unless you have a *real* emergency. Got it?"

"No! Wait!" Before I could say anything more, there was a click, and the line went dead. I exhaled a deep sigh and hung up the receiver. I trudged back to Mitts and Roy, who now had the binoculars.

"Problems?" Mitts asked.

I growled. "Looks like I might have to take the law into my own hands…"

"What do you mean? The cops ain't coming?"

"No." I rubbed my chin, quickly forming another plan.

Suddenly, a gunshot echoed from the direction of the construction site. The three of us jumped.

"What the—" Mitts said.

My heart pounded. *Was that shot for Darin? Or Lu?* I whipped my head to Roy. "Head back down Zerega, park across the street, and be ready to block the entrance."

Roy furrowed his brow. "What? You can't possibly expect my car to hold off two of theirs."

"Just do it! We have to keep them there as long as we can until I can get the boys in blue here."

"But—"

"Mitts! Come with me!" I sprinted down the street.

Mitts kept up with me with his long strides. "What are we doing, Tootsie? I thought you said the cops weren't coming?" he huffed.

"Someone's going to have to make an arrest, so I'll have to keep trying—after I get Darin and Luanda out of there."

Approaching the construction site, Mitts and I edged along the wall. Nearing the driveway. I began to hear distant voices of several men. My heart dropped to my gut. The seconds were ticking away on my one and only opportunity to save Darin and Luanda—if I wasn't already too late. I had to act now, with or without the chief's help. Just me, my gun, my single set of handcuffs, and a small prayer that Beth's morbid prediction from earlier wouldn't come true.

CHAPTER 13

I reached the open driveway of the walled-off construction site. Pressing myself against the wooden privacy fence, I peered around the corner. The construction site looked more like a massive junkyard of abandoned cars, scrap metal, and rubble. Two cars, the brown Caprice and a dark-green Newport, were parked facing each other. Darin and Mel stood facing Curt and four other men I didn't recognize. They must've been Curt's reinforcements. One of the rear passenger doors of the Newport was open, and a pair of cinnamon-toned female legs were sticking out, yellow platform heels tapping the ground nervously. *Luanda?*

"What's happening?" Mitts muttered as he slid into place beside me.

I continued surveying the scene. There were plenty of places to hide. Getting the drop on these guys was going to be another story. I focused the binoculars on the group. Two of the henchmen had their hands inside their blazer fronts. One wore a grey flatcap, and the other stuck out like a piece of broccoli in a candy store in his funky green plaid suit. A third man, short and pudgy, wore a burgundy button-down shirt. His paw was stuffed into a bulging pocket of his white pants. A fourth man who was average height and build wore a dark-brown polo shirt and jeans. He leaned against the driver's side door of the Newport, his arms crossed, and occasionally checked his watch. Mel held his gun at his side, his finger away from the trigger but still too close for my nerves.

"Six men total. At least four are armed," I muttered back to Mitts.

"Well, damn…"

"I'm just going to assume that all of them are armed." I folded the binoculars and stuck them in my coat pocket. Then I pulled out my .38.

He grimaced. "Did I mention how much I *really* hate guns?"

"All the time. Hey, I'm not particularly keen on them either. But unfortunately, criminals don't like to play nice."

"Yeah, yeah." He heaved a heavy sigh. "Well, ain't the first time I brought my fists to a gunfight. Got the scars to prove it. This'll be fun."

"My main priority is getting Luanda and Darin out of there safe. Don't do anything crazy, Mitts."

He cracked a gap-toothed smile. "C'mon. You know me better than that. But if it makes you feel better, I promise not to die."

I groaned. There was no stopping the big lug once he was pumped up on adrenaline. I just hoped he had an inkling of reason left to control his primal urges. "All right. This is it. I'm going in."

"Hey, you be careful, all right? These cats ain't playin'."

I smiled slightly then looked toward the group again. Curt stepped closer to Darin, making sharp gestures with his hands as he spoke. The other men appeared focused on Curt and Darin. I darted inside and ducked behind an abandoned car. Remaining crouched, I crept toward the back of the car, where I had another view of the group.

"…my rules, my way, so long as you work for me!" Curt barked in Darin's face. "You need another reminder?" He prodded his thumb at Mel, who lifted his gun and patted it.

Darin scowled and didn't reply.

"You cost me two hundred grand with that li'l stunt you pulled," Curt continued. "You're gonna work your ass off and earn back my bread."

"Yeah, sure. I'll work. And what are you gonna do for *my* career, huh?" Darin retorted.

"You don't *have* a career without me, you son of a bitch!"

From my vantage point, I had a clear view of the Newport's back passenger seat, where a woman sat with her hands folded in her lap. I sought refuge behind the rusted husk of an old pickup truck, which got me a little closer to the group. Out of the corner of my eye, I spotted a blur of Mitts rushing from the entrance to the back of a large pile of rubble. I returned my gaze to the woman—the stunningly beautiful woman with a physique that made Marilyn Monroe and Jane Russell look like frumpy, potato-sack-wearing eyesores. She had a little Beverly Johnson and Pam Grier wrapped up into all that gorgeous. *Geez Louise. Greg wasn't kidding.*

Luanda fidgeted, her gaze occasionally looking up at Darin and Curt then back down to her hands. Even from twenty feet away, I could tell that look was nervous.

The henchman in green leaned against the back of the Caprice and took out a pack of cigarettes from his blazer. He lit one and took a long drag. Tilting his head back, he exhaled a stream of smoke. Despite the heated chat between Curt and Darin, that guy looked bored out of his mind. There was no way I was going to get Luanda out of that car safely without being spotted.

"Enough talk," Curt said. "You gonna cooperate? Or do I have to make an example outta your girlfriend here?"

Luanda's gaze shot up. Curt gave a small tip of his head to Cigarette Guy. The man nodded, reached inside the car, and yanked her out. She tripped on her long yellow skirt, but she didn't struggle.

Darin took a step forward, but Curt stopped him. "Uh-uh." He pointed at Mel, who held up his gun as a warning.

"Hey, I'm here, like I said I'd be," Darin said. "Lu ain't got nothing to do with us. Let her go."

I clicked off my weapon's safety, then I watched and waited. If they let Luanda go free, half of my problems would be over, and I could focus more of my efforts on getting Darin safe and taking care of Curt and his goons.

"Yeah. Sure. A deal's a deal." Curt casually placed his hands behind his back.

Cigarette Guy shoved Luanda forward, and she stumbled. "Walk," he ordered.

She hesitated, whimpering a little, as she cautiously looked around at the other men, then she slowly made her way toward Darin.

"It's all right, Lu," Darin assured her. "Get out of here."

Her breath hitched. "D-Darin—" Her voice choked.

"Go!" Darin snapped.

She hesitated then took another step.

"Hey, I'm a man of my word. I let her go. She's free..." Curt said. "But for how long?"

"What are you talking about, man?" Darin scrunched his brow.

Curt made a discreet hand gesture behind his back. Cigarette Guy rolled his bogey to one side of his mouth and raised his gun.

Luanda, unsuspecting of the deadly double-cross, fled toward the entrance. I noted Cigarette Guy's steady hand, his finger on the trigger. His face was blank, expressionless. I knew that look—commitment.

He's really going to ice her!

"Get down, Lu!" I popped up from my hiding spot, took aim at Cigarette Guy's center mass, and fired, making a clean shot to the man's chest. He recoiled and collapsed, the gun flying from his hand. Luanda dropped facedown, her arms covering the back of her head. In the chaos, Darin's fighter reflexes kicked in, and he rushed Curt and tackled him to the ground before Curt could even flinch. While the two men tussled, I zipped behind another rusted-out car, making my way closer.

Several gunshots rang out. Stray bullets ricocheted off the car behind me. I winced.

"There! Get her!" Mel shouted.

Footsteps pounded closer along the rocky ground.

I cocked my revolver.

Mitts's animalistic growl echoed off the junk piles. The approaching footsteps stopped, shuffled, and headed in Mitts's direction. I rose from my hiding place and locked my sights on one of the henchmen pursuing Mitts. But out of the corner of my eye, I saw Mel, who had his weapon pointed at me from a distance. I hissed and hunkered back down behind the car. A bullet pinged off the rusted metal.

There was a solid thump, two more ear-ringing gunshots, and a man's groan. My heart stopped a moment. *Mitts...* Unable to see what was going on, I was torn. *No. I need to deal with the source of the problem first.*

I peered around the corner. Darin held Curt's arm down as Curt struggled to grab something out of his blazer. Mel approached them and stopped, his trigger hand wavering as he struggled to get a clear shot without snuffing Curt in the process.

I fired at Mel's feet. He jumped back, head swiveling, and spotted me. Scowling, he pointed his gun in my direction again. Before I could make a move, a flying green-plaid blur smashed into Mel and knocked him flat.

Curt gaped at Mel, who was struggling to push the dead henchman off himself, then looked my way, eyes narrowing.

"Don't make another move, Curt," I said, taking aim.

Curt hesitated. His moment of shock gave Darin his chance, and he landed a solid punch to Curt's jaw. The back of Curt's head bounced against the ground, and his body went limp.

Another shot rang out from Mitts's direction. I swallowed a lump in my throat. "Leave him, Darin. Get Lu to safety!"

Darin lowered his fist and scanned the area. She was gone. He paled. "Where did she go?"

Anxiety rose in my chest. I could only hope and pray that she got out of the area safely. I emerged from my hiding place once more and spotted Mitts. Thankfully, he was still on his feet. The big bear seemed to still be going strong. He held up the pudgy thug by the front of his burgundy shirt and cocked his fist.

Before Mitts could strike, a dark head popped up from behind a ruined cinderblock wall. It was Brown Polo Guy. Light glinted off his chrome weapon. I whirled, my finger tightening on the trigger of my .38, but I was too late. Curt's goon had the drop on Mitts. I couldn't warn my friend in time. My throat tightened. *If I can't save Mitts, at least I can avenge him.*

Suddenly, Luanda charged out from behind an abandoned car, a length of pipe in her hands, and smashed it into the guy's ribs with the force of a Hank Aaron homer. The man howled and collapsed, dropping the gun. Darin hurried over to the guy and finished him off with another one of his goodnight knockouts.

Mel panicked, got back on his feet, and fled for the Caprice. Darin pursued until Mel turned and aimed behind him. Darin leapt out of Mel's line of sight seconds before Mel fired. Then Mel hopped into the driver's seat.

"Don't move, bitch," a man said behind me, followed by the sound of a gun chambering.

My breath hitched. I turned my head slightly. Mr. Flatcap. The only one who hadn't been distracted by Mitts's grand entrance.

"Drop the gun," the henchman ordered.

I did as he said. Mitts and Darin were dealing with Mel's getaway and Lu's safety, so they couldn't help me at this moment.

"I don't know who the hell you are, but you ain't leaving here alive." Mr. Flatcap stepped closer, pressing the gun at my back.

I slowly raised my hands in surrender. "Kill me, and it'll be the end for you too."

"You a cop?"

I didn't answer. No point in wasting my breath on this turkey.

"Okay, then," he continued. "Let's find out."

I shuddered as his grubby hands began frisking me.

"Damn, baby, you're too pretty to be a cop."

I checked the weapon with my peripheral vision. He was holding it relaxed in his right hand for now, as he was most likely being engrossed in his "searching."

"Sorry to disappoint you," I said, before his hands had a chance to travel any lower. In a flash, I spun, grabbing the man's weapon arm and pointing it away. Within seconds, he was down on the ground with a broken wrist, his weapon discarded and the sole of my boot pressed against his throat. While he gagged and made weak attempts to wriggle free, I fished my handcuffs from my coat and secured him against a sturdy, tall metal beam sticking up out of the ground.

Tires screeched ahead, kicking up clouds of dirt and dust. Mel veered toward the exit. I grabbed my gun and ran after the car.

"Watch out, you guys!" I shouted to Darin, Luanda, and Mitts. When I was close enough to the car, I fired at the back window. It shattered, and the car fishtailed to a jerking halt, just as Roy pulled up to block the driveway. While Darin and Luanda made their way out of the construction site, Mitts and I rushed toward Mel's car. Mel lifted his gun and aimed it at Roy, but Roy quickly ducked down in the driver's seat, out of sight.

I reached the driver's-side window of Mel's car and shoved my gun against his cheek. "Don't even think about it."

Mel froze then slowly raised both of his hands, dropping his gun.

"Out. Now," I ordered, taking a small step back and keeping Mel square in my gunsights.

Mel hesitated. Mitts flung the door open, grabbed a handful of Mel's blazer, and yanked him out of the car. I spotted Mel's gun on the floorboard under the steering wheel, but I didn't let my guard down just yet. Who knew how much more that slimy snake was packing?

"Search him, Mitts," I said, keeping my aim locked.

While Mitts patted him down, my ears perked at the sounds of police sirens echoing in the distance. The daily song of the city. However, these sirens sounded close. I sucked in a breath. *Could it be?*

"He's clean," Mitts said.

"No, he's the dirty scum of the earth." I sneered, lowering my gun.

Mel growled. "I can't believe a fucking broad caused all this."

The screaming sirens drew nearer.

"Happy to be of service," I quipped. "You turkeys ain't gonna see the light of day for a long time."

It was Mel's turn to sneer.

Darin and Lu halted halfway to Roy's car as two police cruisers stopped near the entrance. Then a little red Corona topped with a matching spinning dome light appeared. My heart skipped a beat, then a wave of relief swelled through me. *Chief Lewis!* I slid my gun back into my coat.

Two officers jumped out of the cruisers and rushed to the scene. One officer talked with Darin, Lu, and Roy, while the other entered the construction site, his gun drawn. He looked at Mitts and me and paused.

Mitts held up his hands and winced in pain.

"It's all right, sir," I assured the officer. "This man is my friend." I pointed at Mitts. Then I noticed a large spot of blood on the back of his shoulder. I gasped. "Mitts! You're hurt!"

He lowered his hands and grunted, his face still pain-stricken. "Yeah, I'm just feeling it now. Damn, how'd that happen?"

"We'll get you an ambulance."

He hissed. "No, I hate hospitals."

"I'm not going to let you walk around hurt."

"It's just a scratch."

I rolled my eyes. "If you say so."

Chief Lewis, a husky man in a brown suit and tie, stepped out of the Corona and hustled through the entrance. His bushy eyebrows scrunched together as he assessed Curt and the rest of his disabled men strewn out on the ground. He nodded to the officer. "Lenny, take care of these guys."

"Yes, sir." Lenny rushed off.

The chief approached me, his dark face rigid and stern, and his eyes filled with fiery rage.

I swallowed. I knew what he was probably thinking—that I'd gone in way over my head on this one. I knew I had, but it wasn't like I had a choice. Hopefully, he would understand.

Mitts let out a nervous chuckle. "Ah... What's happening, Chief?"

"Hmph. Well, if isn't Mr. Franklin Johnson. Long time no see. You better be staying out of trouble."

"Yes, sir." Mitts let out a hollow chuckle. I could tell how much it irked him that Chief Lewis always addressed him formally, like a school principal addressed a misbehaving kid. But sometimes I wondered if the chief did that deliberately to test Mitts's temper—to see if Mitts was still straight like he'd promised all those years ago after his last run-in with the law.

"I-I'm sorry, Chief," I stammered, attempting to draw the attention away from Mitts. "I... I know you don't want me taking the law into my own hands, but... I had no choice."

"Yeah..." He ran his hand over his thick hair and let out an exasperated sigh. "Are you all right?"

I nodded. "I'm fine. But how did you... I mean, I thought—"

"Yeah, just my luck, you had called when I was in the middle of dealing with that ten-thirty-three report right outside the precinct. Got so serious, we had the bomb squad out there and everything. Thankfully, it was a false alarm. Anyway, when I returned, Stetson mentioned there was 'some crazy stripper broad named Tootsie' who called. I came as fast as I could."

Mitts snorted a laugh. "Stripper? *Tootsie?*"

I shot him a dirty look.

"Anyway," the chief continued, "looks like you cleaned up around here."

"I had help." I made a head gesture to Mitts. "By the way, Chief, I think you're gonna need to call in a couple wagons."

"I don't need no damned 'wagon,'" Mitts countered.

"Not for you. For them." I pointed at the incapacitated men strewn on the ground.

"Already took care of it, Tootsie," Chief Lewis said.

Mitts cringed. "Uh, so, Chief, you're not gonna arrest me, are you?"

Chief Lewis arched an eyebrow. "Why? You protected my number-one ace detective, didn't you? Or is there another reason why I should arrest you?"

Mitts shook his head quickly. "N-No, sir, I'm still straight."

"Good. And you better stay that way."

My smile returned. *Number-one ace detective.* I hadn't heard the chief call me that since I was a kid. "Thanks, Chief. You'll find Curt over there." I pointed at the unconscious manager still sleeping like a baby. "There's enough evidence and witnesses to convict him and his goons."

Chief Lewis nodded. "Yeah. And this time, I'll make sure the case doesn't get thrown out. Good work, Tootsie."

The three of us walked back to the entrance. Chief Lewis sent Andrew to help Lenny with the thugs, and he took over questioning Luanda and Darin. Mitts and I joined Roy by his car.

Mitts put his hand on his shoulder a moment then lifted it, revealing blood on his palm.

I frowned. "Mitts, I really think you should get that checked out."

Roy cringed. "She's right, man. That looks bad."

"I told you no," Mitts said sharply. "I don't do doctors. I'll take care of it. I've been shot plenty of times. This ain't nothin'."

"All right, then," Roy said. "If you think you're too macho to go to a doctor, then I expect to see you working the doors tomorrow night."

Mitts cracked a smile. "Right on. It's a deal."

I sighed and leaned against the front of Roy's car. My nerves were slowly beginning to calm down.

Roy leaned beside me and took my hand in his. The warmth of his hand was comforting. "Tootsie? Are you okay?"

I looked at him. Concern and fluster filled his eyes. "Yeah, I'm fine. What a day."

"Today was absolute bananas, I'll tell ya what. We all nearly got iced today."

"Welcome to my world, Roy."

Roy lifted an eyebrow.   "You still find this detective work 'fun'?"

"Not fun. Interesting and necessary."

"There's nothing 'interesting' or 'necessary' about playing with death every day."

"So long as there are bad people in the world, this job is always necessary. Which also makes it interesting."

Luanda stepped away from the chief and approached us. She smiled at me. "Tootsie, was it?"

She had a cute smile, one that could brighten an entire room. Unfortunately, I was too exhausted to truly bask in her happiness or ogle her beauty, so I simply nodded. "That's me."

"Thank you. I owe you my life," Lu said.

"All in a day's work, Mrs. Miles."

"Please, just call me Lu. You're a friend. A good friend."

I cracked a weak smile.

Chief Lewis and Darin approached. "Tootsie, I'm going to bring those two down to the station to get some paperwork done," the chief said, gesturing to Luanda and Darin. "Then they'll be all yours."

I nodded. "Sure thing, Chief. You need anything else from me?"

"Not now. We'll talk more about this later. The boys and I will take it from here. Go get some rest. You earned it."

Maybe I did earn it, but it didn't make my day feel that good, knowing there would be a couple of men wheeled off to the coroner's instead of the hospital.

CHAPTER 14

By four o'clock, Roy, Mitts, and I had returned to Kronos Lounge. Roy had filled Cheryl and Alex in on everything that had happened. Cheryl had thanked us all profusely, and I'd even managed to get a little gratitude out of the stubborn trainer too. Finally safe and free to go, Cheryl and Alex left the bar and went down to the station to reunite with Luanda and Darin. At Roy's insistent behest, Mitts reluctantly went home to take care of his injuries. I still wished he'd seen a doctor about it, but Mitts's stubbornness rivaled his strength.

I had called Greg from Roy's office, letting him know that Luanda was waiting for him at the Fifty-

Fourth Precinct. I'd never heard a grown man sound so ecstatic in my life. I guess it was understandable, being married to such a stunningly beautiful woman like Lu. Needless to say, Greg had already wired over the rest of my payment, along with a hundred-dollar tip. *Geez Louise, this was definitely one of my most profitable cases.*

There was that limited collector's edition Dick Tracy comic book I'd been itching to get. And maybe I would pick up a jumbo-sized bag of Tootsie Rolls on my next shopping trip. The rest of the money would get stashed away for a rainy day.

After ending the call, I slid off the edge of the desk and sighed. Another case closed after escaping by the skin of my teeth. These cases were getting more and more dangerous, much like this city. My parents were smart to have moved south six years ago before all the political, financial, and social unrest swept through here like a tornado. Mom and Dad were getting older and no longer had the mental strength or patience to endure the nonsense. At least Dad understood why I had to stay here, like he always did, ever since the day he'd given me my first Dick Tracy comic book. I was the apple of his eye, his spunky little girl. He trusted that I had enough street smarts to survive the New York life. Mom, on the other hand, would have preferred that I was more of a lady. *Not today, Mother. Not today.*

Roy returned to his office and sat in his chair behind the desk. He propped his feet on top of the desk and leaned back in his chair. "All done?"

"Yeah. Case closed. Greg is over the moon, being able to see his bombshell wife again."

"Meh. She ain't a bombshell, but she's all right."

I blinked. "All right? That's some jive talk right there..."

"She ain't got nothing on you, Tootsie."

"And how exactly do you figure that? I'm not a model."

"Exactly, and that's what makes you one fine, foxy lady."

I gave him a skeptical look then twisted my lips into a small smile. As much as he got on my nerves, he was charming in his own way. "I'll never understand you, Roy."

"You only need to understand one thing, Tootsie..." Not taking his eyes off me, he swung his legs back to the ground, rose from his chair, and whipped around the desk to stand in front of me. "That I'm crazy about you." He closed his eyes, puckered his lips, and inched his face closer to mine.

I coyly pulled my face away and pressed my finger against his lips. "No, you're just crazy."

He opened his eyes. "After all that happened today and not even one damn kiss?"

"Nah, but I'll take you up on dinner."

His face lit up. "Oh yeah? Finally 'thought about it,' huh?"

"Yeah. I could sure go for a Tootsie Roll milkshake."

"Tonight?"

"Let's make it tomorrow night. I need some sleep. Pick me up around seven."

"Hell yeah. It's a date."

Marlene's Diner was packed at seven thirty on a Friday night. Luanda was back at work, all smiles and laughs, as if yesterday had never happened. Maybe she was just one of those types who found peace in staying busy. To each their own. Still, it was nice to see her smiling face. The wolfish gazes she kept getting from most of her male customers didn't seem to faze her. She was definitely a pro at this. On the other side of the diner, Theresa hustled from table to table, doing an impressive balancing act with her serving tray stacked full of empty dishes. Meanwhile, Nat manned the front counter.

The diner's evening buzz was like white noise to me. There was only one thing that mattered at that moment, and I savored every thick, creamy, chocolatey drop of the best Tootsie Roll milkshake in town. But such delicacies didn't come without their consequences, and mine came in the form of a throbbing brain freeze that felt like a thousand knives being stabbed through my skull. Cringing, I sat back in my booth seat and rubbed my forehead.

Sitting across the table, Roy slid the tall glass away from me. "Don't drink it so fast, or that's what'll happen."

The painful sensation finally ebbing, I pulled the glass back to me. "You know how long I've been waiting to have one of these milkshakes?" I pouted.

He rolled his eyes. "What happened to you being a lady tonight?"

"When I want to be a lady, I make my own rules. And I think a lady can enjoy her milkshake any way she pleases."

"Right..." He cleared his throat. "I was just assuming, since you're dressed all nice for a change instead of in that ridiculous Dick Tracy-wannabe outfit."

"That's my uniform, Roy. But I'm not working now, am I?" Still, I missed my pants, boots, coat, and hat. It wasn't often I had my legs exposed, thanks to my wearing my one burgundy pleated skirt and the brown knitted sweater that my mother had gotten me two Christmases ago. I felt so naked and vulnerable. What if I fell and skinned my knee? And these two-inch, close-toed platform shoes were killing my poor dogs. I could only hope and pray I didn't have to make a fast getaway anytime soon. *How do some women deal with dressing like this every day?* But alas, tonight was a rare, special occasion for many reasons.

"Listen," Roy said. "You always feel like you gotta prove yourself to everyone who tries to put you down. I can dig it. I've felt like that for most of my life. It's why I put all my blood, sweat, and tears into that night club and sit on top as the big boss."

"Is it also why you walk around with all those sexy bombshells on your arm?" I said flatly.

He frowned. "They're just eye candy for the crowd. They don't mean a thing to me."

"Right." I took a noisy slurp of my milkshake.

"It's true. I may not be Superman or even Dick Tracy, but you know what? I'm still somebody, and can't nobody look down their nose at me. Or you, either, Tootsie."

I fiddled with the straw. "What are you trying to say?"

"What I'm trying to say is that you made your mark. People around here respect you. So, for crying out loud, would it kill you to put down the damned gun and act like a lady more often?"

I gave a light shrug. I'd spent most of my life defying society's rules of 'being a lady.' I didn't do it because I had something to prove. I did it because life was so much more fun being the person I wanted to be. Today, I felt like being a lady—my own way. "What you see is what you get, Roy. Take it or leave it," I said.

He snorted and rolled his eyes. "I figured you'd say something like that. Well, I still think you're beautiful either way, so I sure as hell ain't gonna complain."

I smirked and stole a french fry from his fish-and-chips plate. Thankfully, Roy wasn't wearing one of his gaudy pimp suits like he normally did when he was working. A yellow, abstract-printed button-down shirt and dark-brown slacks was as conservative as he got, and that was a-okay with me. I dared say he actually looked handsome for a change, not dressing to impress his next curvy admirer.

Roy had risked his neck for me during this case. Being a lady for him for a change was the least I could do. Besides, I finally had an excuse to try out this new shade of designer nail polish I'd bought from Bloomingdale's. "This has got to be the most we've seen each other during a single week in a long time," I said.

"Tell me about it," Roy said.

"You mean you're not worried about chaos happening at Kronos?"

"Nope. I've got a capable crew to handle things. It's one of the perks of being your own boss, y'know.

You can take off whenever you want." Roy took a bite of his fried cod.

"Oh yeah? So does that mean you're gonna start hanging out with me on all my cases?"

He wrinkled his nose. "I love being around you, Tootsie, but to be perfectly honest, I can't stand your cases. From sitting in a car doing nothing for hours to nearly getting shot at multiple times… that's not for me."

"I could've told you that."

"I wish you'd finally take a break for a change. You're your own boss."

"Ha! Not everyone has the same luxuries as you, Roy."

He arched an eyebrow. "What are you talking about? You know damned well you can do the same thing as me. You just have to learn how to say no."

"Can't say no when I have bills to pay."

"That's why you need a husband," Roy countered.

I snorted. "That's exactly why I *don't* need a husband. A husband means another person, which means another mouth to feed, which means more electricity being used, which means a bigger place to live… more bills."

"Oh, for crying out loud. Fine. No husband, then. Still doesn't mean you can't say no to some of

your clients and take a vacation for yourself
sometime."

"Can't say no to a frantic mother whose child
has run away or a distressed husband whose wife has
gone missing…"

"That's what the police are for."

"The police have bigger fish to fry around this
city."

Before Roy could say any more, Luanda
approached our table, her contagious bright smile
lighting up the diner. "Another milkshake, Detective
Carter?" she asked.

I beamed back. "Oh, I think one will do for
now. And please, call me Tootsie."

"You sure you don't want another? It's on the
house. Nat said so."

I blinked. "W-Well, if you insist…" I slurped
down the rest of my current shake in record time,
bracing for another brain freeze.

Roy groaned. "Shouldn't have said that, Lu.
She's gonna put you guys out of business."

Lu chuckled. "Hey, Nat said Tootsie can have as
many as she wants for saving my life. Oh, and your
meal is on the house, too, Roy."

His expression brightened at that. "Oh? Heh.
Thanks."

"Everything okay with you, by the way?" I asked
her.

Her smile faltered a little as she regarded me again. "Yeah, this is the best thing I can do right now to cope with everything that happened. I swear, if I ever have to stay another night in that awful, flea-ridden motel…"

As it turned out, while I was off on my wild-goose chase, Curt's goons had held Lu hostage at some seedy motel in Brooklyn. She'd been trapped with no way to escape, as men were posted at all the exits, including the fire escape, and she even had a "personal bodyguard" who followed her around like a shadow. Not to mention, they'd tormented her with unwanted sexual advances and threatened her life. How miserable it must've been for her. Part of me regretted that I wasn't able to find her sooner. Maybe I could've spared her some of that suffering.

"Anyway, I don't mind working," Lu continued. "Besides, I'm helping Greg build up our vacation fund again."

I cringed then rubbed the back of my head. "Uh, yeah… about that…"

"Hey, that vacation isn't going anywhere. Tapping into our funds to hire you was necessary and money well spent. I will always be grateful for you and your friends risking your lives for me."

"We're just glad you're safe." Roy nodded.

"Thank you." Lu's smile returned. "I'll go get you that milkshake, Tootsie." She spun and went behind the front counter.

I propped my elbow on the table and rested my cheek in my palm as I watched her whip up another milkshake in a fresh glass. "She sure is nice."

"Yeah," Roy said absently. "Let's just hope she doesn't get into any more trouble next time."

"Hopefully, there won't be a next time."

The entrance door swung open, and Cheryl walked in, dressed in dark-denim bell-bottom jeans and a cute, multi-colored striped sweater. She wore a wide grin as she strode up to the front counter. She looked like a completely different woman now—excited and carefree—compared to the worried, defensive mess I'd first met. Cheryl chatted with Lu. Moments later, Lu set down a can of whipped cream and looked at her friend, wide-eyed. Her smile grew.

Cheryl said something else and held out her hand, nodding. Then Lu squealed. Finally, the both of them went into a squealing fest, like two excited high school girls. I bolted upright in my seat.

The buzz of the diner lowered as patrons turned to stare.

Lu and Cheryl looked around, then Lu beamed and waved her arms. "My friend just got engaged!" she announced.

Roy and I exchanged raised eyebrows. *Talk about a happy ending,* I thought.

Light claps, whistles, and cheers came from the patrons, then they returned to their meals and conversations.

Theresa disappeared through the double doors to the kitchen with her tray of dirty dishes, then she reappeared seconds later with an empty tray. She rushed to Lu and Cheryl and joined in the celebration.

Nat finished ringing up a customer. "Hey, hey, hey! After work, ladies!" She pointed at Lu and Theresa. "Table Five needs more napkins. Get to it! And, Cheryl, don't go starting trouble around here just 'cause you're off today." Nat cracked a smile.

Cheryl laughed. "You know I wouldn't do that." After saying goodbye to Lu and Theresa, Cheryl approached our table. "Mind if I join you guys?"

"Be our guest." I scooted over. "Love the sweater, by the way."

"Isn't it cute? I got it on sale at Macy's."

Lu returned to our table with a brand-new milkshake for me, topped with whipped cream and a bright-red cherry. "Here you go!"

Grinning, I greedily pulled the tall glass closer. "Swell. Thanks."

Lu nodded, cast another excited smile at Cheryl, then zipped to another table.

"Congratulations on your engagement, by the way," Roy said while I shamelessly sucked down half my milkshake through a straw.

Cheryl sighed dreamily and splayed her left hand on the table, revealing a gold ring with the biggest, shiniest diamond I'd ever seen. "Can you believe it? Darin spent pretty much all his winnings from that last fight on this ring. It was such a surprise. I was definitely not expecting him to propose this morning."

"He sure doesn't mess around, huh?" I laughed.

"You can say that again. Right after I said yes, he went off to the gym. But he told me to meet him here around eight o'clock tonight."

"Sounds like a date to me."

Cheryl shrugged. "Maybe. I mean, this *is* where we first met. Maybe he wants to make it a little extra special. For a fighter, he's quite the romantic."

The entrance door opened again, and two men walked in. "Well, speak of the devil..." I nodded toward Darin, who was with a dark-haired, middle-aged man in a suit.

Roy looked over his shoulder. "Huh. Who's that fancy-looking cat with him?"

Cheryl popped up from her seat. "I don't know, but I'm going to find out." She hurried over to Darin and threw herself into his arms, kissing him deeply.

While the two of them chatted, the suited man looked around, a hint of anxiousness in his blue eyes.

What's his bag? I narrowed my gaze, trying to remember where I'd seen him before. I almost never forgot a face. I couldn't pinpoint his, however. I assessed the rest of his dark-grey suit and the complementing red tie.

Red tie. Wait a minute…

My body tensed. I slowly balled my hands into fists.

"What's wrong, Tootsie?" Roy asked.

I tightened my jaw. "That man. I've seen him before. At Sunnyside Garden Arena. I think he might be another one of Curt's guys."

Roy blinked. "What!"

Cheryl tugged Darin toward our table, and Mr. Red Tie followed. She clapped her hands together. "Guys! Guess what? Darin has an agent! A real, honest-to-goodness legit agent!"

I swallowed a lump in my throat. "Another one? Already?"

Darin smiled slightly. "Hey, I learned my lesson." He gestured to Mr. Red Tie. "This is Nicholas Jacobsen of Jacobsen and Associates Sports Agency. One of the top sports agencies on the East Coast. Can you believe I ran into this guy at Primo's this morning? He said he was looking for me. Looking for *me!* Can you believe it? A lot of famous pro athletes have been represented by Nick's agency." He gestured to me. "Nick, this is Detective Tootsie Carter."

Nick did a double take, then his dark eyebrows shot up. "You again. So you're the woman he's been going on about. Detective, huh?"

I frowned and held my head high. "That's right."

Darin looked curiously between the two of us and wrinkled his brow. "Wait, you two already met?"

"You could say that," I said, not taking my eyes off Nick. "What were you doing that night at the arena?"

Nick shrugged. "Scouting, what else? After Darin walked out with that massive win, I called one of my associates to have them dig up some more info about him."

The telephone. So that's who he was talking to.

"Darin's a man of value and potential," Nick continued. "He's looking for a comeback, and I plan to give it to him."

I narrowed my eyes. "Sounds like something Curt would say."

"Hey, Nick's the real deal," Darin assured. "Alex and I were up in his Midtown Manhattan office on the thirty-second floor all day today, talking about my future. Even Alex could vouch for him. And he never vouches for anyone."

"Well, Curt managed to weasel his way around without Alex knowing," I said.

"Yeah, well, Alex ain't letting that happen again. You can bet on it."

"Hmm…" I still wasn't thoroughly convinced.

Nick gave me a reassuring smile. "I know about Zanetti and the crooked racket he was caught up in, Detective. He ruined a lot of good athletes' careers with his scams he had going. You did us all a favor by getting him and his friends off the street."

My gaze swiveled back and forth between Nick and Darin, and I scowled. "All right, Mr. Jacobsen. I'll take your word for it that you're straight. But if I hear anything about Darin being in trouble again, you and I are gonna have a little chat. Can you dig it?"

Nick chuckled, putting his hands up in surrender. "Hey, hey. I promise you, I run a legit business. Ask any professional athlete or sports organization. Nice meeting you, Ms. Carter." He cleared his throat and looked to Darin. "I need to go. Call me when you guys get back to Philadelphia."

"Will do." Darin nodded.

After Nick left, Cheryl wrapped her arm around Darin's waist. "So, baby, are we gonna make the most of this night, or what?"

"Of course." Darin kissed her.

I smiled at them. "I'm happy for you two. Live life to the fullest."

Darin winked. "We will. Thanks, both of you. And tell Mitts thanks, also, when you see him. My life's been turned upside down in just a few days."

"It's been interesting, to say the least," I said.

We said our goodbyes to Darin and Cheryl, and they sat together in a tiny booth at the back of the diner. Luanda took the opportunity to zoom over their way, while Theresa was idly wiping down a nearby table but standing by to eavesdrop on more gossip.

Roy propped his elbow on the table, leaning his cheek against his fist. He sighed. "Will that ever be us, Tootsie?"

I stirred my milkshake with the straw. "Maybe one day, when there's no more crime in this city."

His eyes dulled. "In other words, never."

"Hey, Dick Tracy worked all his life."

"Oh yeah? Well in case you forgot, your beloved Dick Tracy was also married, and sometimes he did take breaks."

"Yeah, and poor Tess got kidnapped more times than you could count. And even *she* knew that being married to someone like Dick Tracy wasn't all it was cracked up to be."

"That's fiction. This is reality. Things will be different between you and me. I won't get kidnapped, and I damn sure won't have second thoughts about marrying you."

I shook my head. "It's not in the cards right now, Roy. We lead two completely different lives. If you really care about me, then you'll respect my choice. This city is my home, and it needs someone like me to help clean it up."

He looked at me deeply for several moments, frowning. "It's our home." His lips tugged upward to a small smile. "I admire you, Tootsie. You have a big heart. This city does need someone like you. But whenever you're finally ready to take that break, I'll be there for you."

Grinning, I held up my milkshake. "I'll drink to that."

M. RAVENEL

M. Ravenel is the author of the *Plainclothes Tootsie* mystery series featuring a tough, snarky private eye from 1970s New York City. When not writing, reading, or working out, Ravenel enjoys watching Golden Age hard-boiled and noir detective films. Ravenel may sometimes be spotted wearing a signature trench coat and fedora while penning the next *Plainclothes Tootsie* story on a typewriter-inspired keyboard.